SHANNON'S GAMBLE

A gripping, action-packed thriller

PAUL BENNETT

Nick Shannon Thrillers Book 7

Joffe Books, London
www.joffebooks.com

First published in Great Britain in 2023

Cover Design by Nick Castle

ISBN: 978-1-80405-872-5

AUTHOR'S NOTE

For every bet you place, whether it be online, at a betting shop, casino or whatever, the bookmaker takes a margin (their profit) by the beneficial setting of the odds of an event happening. Think of the zero on a roulette wheel. The safer a bet, such as in a casino where the odds on the spin of a roulette wheel are known, the margin might be as low as three per cent: for less predictable events — a bet on a horse winning a race or a team winning a football match — the margin might be ten per cent or more. This margin means that in the long run you will never beat the bookie — you will lose. Unless you cheat.

CHAPTER ONE

I would not be bullied. I would be polite. I would be patient. But I would not be bullied. The man at the head of the table had a ferocious reputation as a bully, for throwing his not inconsiderable weight around and I would let him wash over me. I would not rise to the bait, I would not be cowed. That was the theory.

Never has a business benefitted so much from a corpse. After the death of the Home Secretary, and my involvement in it, the business of Shannon Investigations, fraud detectives, had boomed. We had acquired a reputation for not taking prisoners and no one, no matter how high, would be free from the law: clients wanted our imprimatur for their businesses; the Shannon stamp of approval. As a consequence, we had a full order book and could turn down those with whom we did not want to work. So, this man had better be careful or I could easily shake his hand and walk away. Well, I'd offer him my hand: whether he shook it or not was his decision.

The act resulting in the Home Secretary's death had provided me with justice for the man who had crippled my sister in the hit-and-run that had mown her down and had seen me, Nick Shannon, spending seven years at Her Majesty's pleasure for assisted suicide, although I failed to see what pleasure she might have derived from it. She was too nice a lady for that.

I had driven to this skyscraper in East London, been stopped at a barrier, checked through an elaborate security process including patting me down, taken the lift to the top floor and now entered a large room with a panoramic view of the City of London where two people sat at a long table of black ash with chrome legs, although the second person was a shadow around the bulk of Sir Gerald Campion: he was a bit player standing in the wings while Campion gave his soliloquy. Campion was the head of Zeus, a multibillion enterprise with tentacles stretching from all forms of media — hard copy and electronic — satellite TV and various online businesses. Today's meeting concerned the gambling sector of his empire.

According to his official biography, Campion was aged sixty, but he looked much older than that from the ravages of a life poorly lived. He had deep bags under his eyes and his forehead was lined from the permanent frown he wore. His nose was red and his face flushed by broken blood vessels. This was the face of a heavy drinker.

His suit was handmade and fitted his heavy frame like a glove — gauntlet was probably a more appropriate word. He had on a white shirt and a red-striped tie that indicated to the knowledgeable to which exclusive club he belonged. I couldn't see below the table, but our researches showed that he was below average height at five foot eight.

Campion stared at me, making his initial assessment and putting me in some stereotypical box in his category of underlings. He consulted his watch. Took it off and laid it flat on the table in front of him. 'You have five minutes and no more,' he barked. 'Tell me the most important point you want to make.'

'Three thousand pounds a day,' I said. 'Plus expenses, plus VAT plus ten per cent of any frauds found.' I paused. 'Four minutes saved.'

Campion leaned back in his chair, looked at me, rocked forward, gave a bellowing laugh and slapped the table with his palm. 'I like you, Shannon. A man after my own heart.

You must come for dinner. I'll get my people to talk to your people. Bring a guest. Do you have a wife?'

'Not yet,' I said, 'but I have what they class as a significant other, although you won't thank me for bringing her.'

'Harridan, is she?' he asked.

'Far from it, although she can give as good as she gets. The reason why you won't like me introducing her to you is that she is the most beautiful woman you will ever have seen. After meeting Cherry, all women will pale into insignificance.'

'I look forward to welcoming you both.' He stood up and walked to the door. He was shoeless. He turned and then looked at the other man. 'Make it happen,' he said.

As the door closed behind Campion, the other man said, 'Phew!'

'Phew indeed,' I added. 'Good summary.'

He stood up and extended his hand. I walked to the table, shook his hand and sat down. 'David Shapiro,' he said. 'Call me David, if you like.'

Shapiro had on a dark grey suit with a pink shirt and red tie — must be colour blind. But at least he wasn't wearing the standard dark blue suit and white shirt that was the uniform of ninety per cent of male businessmen. There was a handkerchief in the colours of the Ukrainian flag in the top pocket of his jacket: he went up in my estimation. He was slim, had black hair cut fashionably short and what looked like a Mediterranean tan, natural rather than from a spray can. This guy had roots.

'I know what you're going to ask me,' he said. 'Yes, he is always like that. Worse in fact. You got off lightly. He must like you, for sure. And as for an invitation to dinner, I've never heard that before. But,' he said, 'formalities. Let me introduce myself. I'm CEO of Zeus — the holding company that owns everything. Coffee?'

'That would be good,' I said. 'Thank you.'

He picked up a telephone and made the order — espresso for me and a latte with oat milk for himself. Interesting.

3

'What's with the socks?' I asked.

'Gout,' Shapiro said. 'Hard to get his shoes on without causing pain. Makes him even more irascible.'

While we waited for the coffee, I sensed an awkwardness in him.

'My turn,' I said. 'I know what you are going to ask. It's ever-present. Yes, prison was like a layer of hell, but I made lifelong friends and had a Damascene moment. Before my sister's death, I was about to start a Masters, looking at the mathematical economics of games theory, and a career in academia. And here I stand before you, prosperous and in love. A man with nearly everything.

'When I was on remand in Brixton, it was ruled by a thug called Freddie Ronson. He was the main man. He ruled the roost. He thought he could do anything to me. One day — in the showers, naturally — he tried to rape me. He was bigger than me, heavier than me. In a fair fight, I was powerless. So, like my cellmate, Arthur, taught me, I fought dirty. I used two fingers on my left hand to blind him. He got revenge. The morning I was due to move to Chelmsford — Category 3, low risk — he bribed two of the bent screws to put those two fingers in the jamb of the steel door and slam it shut.' I placed my left hand on the table and showed him the thumb and two fingers that remained. 'So, I have almost everything plus a permanent reminder of the past.'

'I'm sorry,' Shapiro said. 'I didn't mean to evoke painful memories.'

'What I have, I would gladly give it all up to have my sister alive and well again. Maybe not give it all up, upon more consideration. Love is a great healer. Now where the hell is that coffee? I'm full of no caffeine!'

He laughed, thinking that the words were mine, not knowing that I had lifted them from a Raymond Chandler novel I'd read in my youth and waited all this time to speak them.

Miraculously, as if someone had heard my prayers, the door to the room opened and in came a smartly-dressed woman in black, in her thirties, bearing a tray. She nodded at Shapiro and placed the tray between us. She withdrew and we helped ourselves. Only the fact that it came in cardboard mugs broke any illusion of luxury. He looked at me and shook his head.

'The only coffee,' he began to apologise, 'outside of lunch in the canteen, is via a machine and it is truly foul. Sir Gerald watches every penny.'

'I understand. Thank you for the honour of a takeaway.'

I sipped the coffee and smiled at him. He smiled back. This was a person with whom I could do business.

'We did some background research on you,' he said. 'The fact that you were interested in games theory hit the right note — it's our gambling business, Zeusbet, that we want to talk about. We're losing money, and that shouldn't happen.'

'That would be the only bookmakers I've ever heard of that hasn't made a profit,' I said. 'You might have a bad day at the track or a bad spell of the roulette wheel, but the odds are in the bookmakers' favour. In the long run the bookies always show a profit.'

'Except us, it seems. Sir Gerald doesn't like losing money. The auditors have signed off the accounts and didn't pick anything up. It needs a different approach, so we thought of you. If we can't turn around the Gambling Division, Sir Gerald will divest himself of it. That will hurt him, though. He is like a spoilt brat: if he can't win, he won't want to play. You are going to help him save face as well as money. If it all works out, he will ask you to do the same at our other two divisions.'

'Any guesses on where the losses stem from?' I asked.

'It's not the casinos — some of them are doing well — but you should check them out, so we know why there are differences across our sites and maybe learn from them. It's the Betting Shops and Online trading where the worst shortfalls in profit are. What will you need from us?'

'Access to your accounts and computer system and the key personnel we will need to talk to, together with any security passes and so on — I'll need three sets of everything to allow another two of my colleagues to take part, too. Probably good to have a helper who can explain the systems and, more importantly, do frequent trips to the coffee shop.'

'I've already lined someone up,' he said. 'Please be gentle with him. He's my son.'

Oh hell, I said to myself. That was all I needed. A spy in the camp. Everything I did reported straight back to Daddy. What would he make of my often unconventional methods?

Too late now. Let the game begin.

CHAPTER TWO

He was waiting for me outside the room in the small lobby area by the lifts. He got up from a sofa and walked towards me, extending his hand. I studied him and made my first impressions — first impressions are rarely wrong, I've found, or if they are, few people admit them.

He was my height — six foot three — but there the similarities finished. His hair was blond, long and straight whereas mine was brown and wavy: his eyes blue, mine green. He was around twenty-two, I was thirty-eight — an age gap that might get in the way? He was wearing a tailored three-piece suit in light grey over a blue shirt, no tie. I was in the obligatory client uniform that I should really upgrade: off the peg, dark blue suit, white shirt and subdued tie — not striped and representing some school, university or club. Overall, though, he was the most handsome — no, make that beautiful — man I had seen for many a year. He would be a babe magnet. Could that be useful?

'Valentine,' he said, shaking my hand limply. He was nervous. 'Don't ask. Valentine Shapiro.'

'Nick Shannon,' I replied. 'Call me Nick, or just plain Shannon. Mister just gets in the way. Let's go somewhere to talk. Anywhere you can recommend?'

'Follow me.'

He led me down a floor and into some kind of cafeteria. *Some kind of* because it did not have any degree of attraction that would invite someone to stay for long — quick in, serve yourself, eat, back to work, there being nothing else to do. It had wide windows on two sides providing views over the City of London and Docklands as per the floor above; that was the best bit. As if to discourage customers, the strip lights glared down with a sharp flicker. The walls were painted a bilious yellow and had lots of tables with dark wooden tops. It all had a sad vibe and, consequently, didn't have more than a few people inside. It was still early in the lunchtime break so I gave it the benefit of the doubt that everyone would swarm in on the dot of one. Or maybe not. As with most things, time would tell.

The saving grace was that there was a proper coffee machine complete with a barista. Expensive, compared to the high street shops, but money well spent. We got coffees, Valentine paying by swiping a card through a machine and went to sit by a window seat.

'First off,' he said. 'I'll need to get you a card so you can buy anything when I'm not around.'

'What do you do when you're not around for me?'

'This and that,' he said.

'Good to know. That's my curiosity sated.' I paused to let the irony sink in. It went over his head. 'Now, what do you really do? What's your role in this empire?'

'I'm a graduate trainee — Dad didn't want any talk of nepotism about my appointment, so it was start at the bottom of the executive ladder.'

'Many graduate trainees, are there?' I asked.

'So far, just me.'

No nepotism there, then.

'I float between the work teams, helping where I can,' Valentine said. 'It's easier to understand if I take you through the structure. Hold there.'

He got up from the table and went back to the coffee machine area and took a napkin from the dispenser. He spread it out, took out a ballpen and started to draw.

'Here we are, Sir,' he said.

'No sir. Like I said, Nick or Shannon.'

'Sorry,' he said, blushing.

'Ten out of ten for the blush. Zero out of ten for following orders. Must do better. Now, carry on.'

He went back to the napkin and drew a box at the start of what would become a pyramid. 'This is my dad, CEO of the group, Zeus. Ultimately, everything stems from him and is accountable to him — except that Sir Gerald can't help but interfere. Below him, there are CEOs of the three divisions — Publishing of newspapers and magazines, Satellite TV or Broadcasting and Gambling. They each have a CEO. If we move down the tree in the Gambling Division, there are three departments — Casinos, Betting Shops and Online — each with their own head. Down from there are the computer people and the experts for each sport. Working alongside the experts, there is a second layer of mavens, called watchers. Most of the odds are set by algorithms in the computer central system. The experts can override the computer if they have new information — key striker goes down with a last-minute injury and can't play, for example. It's the job of the watchers to check the experts and verify their work. A policing role best sums it up.'

Very succinct. Maybe he wasn't a blond bimbo after all.

'Well done, Valentine. So where do we start?'

'I've set you up a meeting tomorrow with the Head of the Gambling Division and then you can work down from there — you won't get much cooperation without his approval.'

'Presumably, you'd like to sit in on any meetings? Report back progress to your father?'

'I won't snitch on you, if that's what you are worried about. I'll only report those things you want mentioned. I guess, too, that my father is looking for me to learn from you. Good experience. Help me grow. I won't let him or you down.'

'OK,' I said. 'I'll try to include you in all my findings and suspicions. One slip and you'll get nothing further. Understood?'

'Cool,' he said. I would have liked something a bit more definite than *cool*, but it was early days.

'So,' I said, 'what do we do until we can start talking to people? Any ideas?'

'How would you like a bet?' he said.

'Cool,' I replied.

* * *

There being limited parking where we were going, Valentine called a taxi and we set off for Leytonstone High Street to the east of London. It seemed like a high street you would see replicated across the country. There were chain coffee shops, small supermarkets, estate agents and corner shops. Right next to the betting shop there was a pawn shop, as if they had been designed together as a pair to feed customers from one to another. The only other notable exception to the cloning of shops across the country was a pie and mash café, a board outside proudly proclaiming jellied eels, too. I wasn't tempted.

Betting shops had changed since the last time I had entered one in my university days. Gone was the thick cloud of smoke, the lino floor littered with cigarette butts and discarded losing betting slips, the long shelves for writing out the bets, the sporting pages of riders and runners taped on the walls and the absence of seating. This shop was smoke free and carpeted. There were comfortable chairs in the middle of the room and a long counter for placing your bets. In addition to the desks for writing out bets, there were self-service terminals. All mod cons. Instead of the newspapers and chalkboards of odds, there were computer screens everywhere. There were customers unashamed of what they were about to do, risking the week's housekeeping. To keep the customers occupied between bets, there were three slot machines, every one with a punter pouring coins dexterously into the slot. It was a whole new universe.

Valentine waved at one of the cashiers and got her attention — that had been unusual in the past, too — to open the door to the back-room offices. He flashed his blue card that had his name, but no picture. The woman opened the glass door and saw his name. She couldn't have acted more quickly. We were led away from the cashiers' desks with their multiple screens and cash registers into a room where we were greeted by a tall woman of about forty in a black trouser suit and heels similar to what a female referee in a snooker match would wear — only the white gloves were missing. Her black hair was swept up and held back by a scrunchy and she radiated an aura of efficiency. Her name was Sandra and she motioned us to sit down in two chairs at a table where she took up a seat. On the desk in front of her were two computer screens. Her eyes flickered between them and us.

Valentine fluttered his long eye lashes. She would be putty in his hands.

'How can I help you, Mr Shapiro?' she said to Valentine.

'Mr Shannon here is doing some work for my father—' I wondered how often he played the father card '—and needs to get a feel of the business. He wonders whether you could take him through the process.'

'I'd be eternally grateful,' I said, trying some of the Shannon charm. Hopeless: she only had eyes for Valentine.

'Well, Mr Shannon,' she said, 'let me show you the most important piece of equipment. Equipment that allows everything to function.' She got up and walked to the back wall. She picked up a wire. 'Nothing functions without this. Via this, the odds are transmitted constantly for each race as bets are laid. Those odds are displayed on the monitors for our customers. They fill out a form — that's the only thing that we haven't computerised. They take it to one of the cashiers who takes the money — either cash or card — and inputs it into the system — the original form is kept in case there is some dispute. If the customer wins, the amount of money to be handed over is calculated by the system. The odds are constantly being updated as bets are made. Any large last-minute bets are identified and rejected if there's a suspicion of something out of the ordinary going on or allows us to lay them off — essentially putting bets with Betfair or the other betting companies to reduce our risk.'

The mention of cash wetted my lips. Where cash is involved, there's always someone who will be tempted to get their hands on it. There is an allure about cash that overrides any reservations about fraud.

'How much of the takings are in cash?' I said.

'The amount in cash has been declining over the last couple of years, but there are always some who don't trust cards or don't want items showing on their bank account or credit card statement — there's still a stigma about gambling. And there's a steady stream who pawn something and can't wait to spend it.'

'What sort of amounts are we seeing before you worry about where the cash came from or where it's going?' I said.

'No limit,' she replied.

'Surely you could be helping someone to launder money?' I said, trying to keep the shock out of my voice.

'If they have money, we gladly take it,' she said. 'Anyway, the customer could simply place smaller amounts in multiple bets. What's the problem?'

If she couldn't see the problem, then that was the problem.

'And is this company policy?' I asked.

'That view stems from the top,' she said. 'I'm just following orders.'

How often had I heard those views? They were a licence to act without conscience. A shrug of the shoulders to consequences.

'Let's test the system,' I said. 'Come on, Valentine. Time to show your worth.'

We walked to the office door, stood by the outer door and waited for one of the cashiers to unlock it. Back in the main customer area, I looked at the screens. It was a quiet day with the only racing taking part at Wincanton, a rural track in Devon: there wouldn't be many bets cast, and that, fortunately, fitted my purpose. I looked at the odds and found an unfancied 20/1 shot called Danny's Boy.

There were only five customers and I took out my wallet and gave a twenty-pound note to each of them. 'Take the odds on Danny's Boy in the next race. Bet each way — those finishing in the top three. Two bets at ten pounds each.'

Let me for a moment give you some background on the esoteric ways of the betting world. There are two ways to wager. Take the odds at the time of your bets — for those who think the odds would shorten and, therefore, be in your favour as everything is — or take the odds when the race starts, the exact opposite.

While they started filling out the necessary forms, I picked up a bunch of around twenty forms from the pile. 'You know what to do?' I said to Valentine. 'Ten pounds each way on each. Start writing.'

It didn't take long before we started queueing at the cashiers' counter. I could see the cashiers wondering what was going on. I watched the screens as the bets were transferred up the system to be checked and recorded. The odds were coming down. By the time all the bets were placed, the odds had shortened to 16/1. The algorithm had noticed the unusual flurry and had kicked in. An expert and/or a maven from the watchers would now be examining the bets and making a decision on what to do — they would still have time before the start of the race — void all the bets and hand back the money to all of us, lay off some of the money to other bookies, but it was small bets and unlikely to cause a flurry, or just let everything ride.

There was a spark of electricity as the screens went from the odds view to the race live. Danny Boy took the lead — never a good sign as it often caused tiredness as the race progressed. He hung on grimly but was passed in the final furlong: he was a creditable third place, giving us a win on every ten-pound bet of around fifty pounds. The gods smiled at us. Long may that last.

'What have we just learned, Valentine?' I said.

'That it's possible to beat the system, albeit in a small way.'

'At the risk of sounding patronising,' I said, 'well done, my lad. You're learning. And if there's one way to beat the system, there could be others. And we might be able to scale things up to something sizeable. Someone hasn't thought everything through. OK, we were lucky and we don't know how much we could get away with, but it all seems positive. From my point of view, that is; from the point of view of Zeus, negative.'

'This is fun,' he said.

'And this is only the beginning,' I said. 'Long may it last. Now, tomorrow. We need to speak to the Head of the Gambling Division and then, as soon as possible, to the heads of the three subdivisions — Online, Casinos and Betting Shops. I doubt we can get all that until after a couple of days. We have to do it in that order, otherwise people will clam up. I'd also like to visit a casino, and one that is still making a profit. Is there one nearby?'

'The closest one is at Lakeside, part of the big shopping centre. Shouldn't take more than half an hour to get there.'

'There'll be three of us. It will be a good opportunity for you to meet the team informally. Fix it up for tomorrow evening. OK, do your homework tonight — think on another thing you should have learned.'

'Any clues?' he asked.

'Life doesn't come that easy, Valentine. And that, my friend, is another lesson in itself.'

CHAPTER THREE

A converted wharf building set in Docklands close to Island Gardens and the foot tunnel under the Thames to Greenwich was our home and office combined. It was five storeys high, and we used every inch of it.

The ground floor was the main working area with a large office for me, two smaller offices for staff and a panoramic sitting area looking out on the river. The first floor was for getting together as a group when we were not working. The second was Norman's floor — Norman was a convicted embezzler with whom I shared a cell in Chelmsford. Whatever the circumstance, whatever the situation, Norman always came out on top. A true mentor with a knowledge of fraud unsurpassed by most professionals. The significant other who resided with him was Morag, a woman of around sixty from the poshest area of Edinburgh with a lovely trill to her voice. We had recruited her from her job as the PA to the Chief Constable of the Mid-Anglia police force after the death of the Home Secretary and her boss being kicked out. Morag managed the administration of the company and was ably assisted, now that the business had grown so much, by our latest recruit, Beryl, from her position as PA to the head of a firm of solicitors until he was poisoned. Sounds like I'm always collecting dead bodies, doesn't it?

The third floor had been recently taken over by Anji, our trainee. Anji added the spice to our team. She's young, very pretty — second only in the beauty stakes to Cherry — and keeps us up to date with the modern way of doing things and, in particular, among the young. She has a degree in Economics from Exeter and, not being able to get a job in these hard times, did some work as a pole dancer to earn some money to pay the rent. Her normal dress was as feisty as she was, but she could put on camouflage when she was with a client, including a pair of glasses with clear lenses.

The top floor was for me and Cherry. I had worked alongside her in the Fraud Squad, when I was seconded there, where she had risen to the rank of Chief Inspector. Our relationship could be best described as tempestuous, until the death of my former partner, Arlene. What had been love-hate had become love-love.

Our last member, who did not live with us, was Arthur. He was an ex-wrestler fighting under the name of Arthur 'Dangerous' Duggan. Arthur had been my cellmate in Brixton. He taught me self-defence and how to survive while doing your time. He was six foot five and built like a bear — and like all bears, could be cuddly, too. Arthur had had to give up wrestling because his brain worked too slowly and he couldn't remember the rehearsed moves for the fight — opponents got regularly hurt, until no one would wrestle with him. He had been incarcerated in Brixton for collecting what he was told was a debt, but was in reality protection money. He mainly worked as a door steward — the unthreatening name for a bouncer — and some private protection.

So that was our motley crew.

We were gathered at the end of the working day in the communal area on the first floor where we were about to review the day and plan what to do tomorrow and the next few days. Beryl and Morag had produced our drinks and we sat on the four Chesterfields in the room. Except Anji — she sat cross-legged in the floor with her trademark over-the-knee biker boots, skater's skirt and crop top that showed off her slim stomach with the stud in her belly button. She was taking small sips of a gin and tonic over lots of ice and a slice of lemon — that would last her the whole evening.

Cherry was still in her work clothes of a black trouser suit and white top and she reclined on the sofa with her legs tucked under her, looking a million dollars. Her natural beauty was enhanced by her coffee-cream skin and her bone structure was perfect. She'd tied her black wavy hair up with a plain gold band. Her eyes were the deepest black and her smile was electric.

'Will you start off, Cherry?' I said. 'How long before you can wrap up the Lifestone project?'

Lifestone was a building company that had seen profits slump. They had called us in for advice. Sure enough, someone was on the fiddle. We would usually pass the file over to the Fraud Squad, but it was up to the client whether we took that step. Most chose not to because of the adverse publicity it would attract.

'Anji and I have been through a draft report, and there's just a few additions and revisions to make. Be finished after the day after tomorrow, as long as nothing else comes up.'

'Anything juicy?' Norman asked, curiosity and the interest of our bottom line of profit getting the better of him.

'Two things,' said Cherry. 'The old credit control scam and . . .'

'Not yet,' I interrupted. 'Well, Anji,' I said. 'Let's see what you have learned so far. Explain the credit control scam.'

Anji gave a sigh. 'The fraudster is the credit controller, the person responsible for chasing up late payments. He, or she, says that a debt is irrecoverable and gets it written off in the accounts. He then contacts the debtor and offers a hefty discount if they pay up in cash. He pockets the money. The debtor is happy, the credit controller is happy — only the company loses out.'

'OK. Looking good, Anji. Continue please, Cherry.'

'Another small scam,' she said. 'Teeming and lading . . .'

'I get the picture,' said Anji. 'You don't have to ask me. Teeming and lading is usually pulled by the accounts manager. The scenario runs something like this. The perpetrator is short of money. Let's go for the feminine this time. She, the accounts manager, is short of money. She takes some from the payments coming in and needs to cover it until she can repay. Life doesn't work that way. She can't repay, so she takes money from the next day's receipts and puts it against what she already has taken to balance the books. The most common perpetrators of teeming and lading are gamblers. The gambler always loses. The sums gets bigger and bigger until there's no chance of hiding them. Handcuff time.'

'And here endeth the second lesson,' I said. 'Let's come to the Zeus project. Initially, and this is only day one, I think we will need to put four people under the microscope — the CEO of the Gambling Division and the three Heads for Casinos, Betting Shops and Online Betting. I could do with Anji's time from tomorrow, and then yours, Cherry, when you are free. I'm going to need surveillance, too. Arthur, can I put you down for mobile spying in your white van? At six foot five you're a teeny bit noticeable for street work, so I'll get someone else to cover on foot.'

'Who is?' said Norman.

'The guy at the Abacus Detective Agency — "Abacus, you can count on us!" — did a pretty good job on the Ackroyds' case. I'd be happy to run with him.'

'Costs?' said Norman.

'Won't be expensive,' I said.

'Don't forget,' Norman said. 'It's a wise man that knows the value of his own product. You get what you pay for.'

'Let's give him a shot.' I said. 'He could be a good asset in the future if this works out. Tomorrow, I'd like to take Anji with me during the day and, if the arrangements have been made, Anji, Cherry and myself will be going to a casino. Anything else from anyone?'

Morag pulled a face. 'You're not going to like this,' she said. 'Campion's PA rang. You're invited to dinner.'

'What is there I shouldn't like?' I asked.

'The PA was very insistent. As I said, you're not going to like it.'

'Spit it out, Morag,' I said.

'They dress for dinner.'

CHAPTER FOUR

We travelled to the Zeus complex in the BMW M3, which could hold its own against most sports cars. I had the dealer to take off all the M3 badges and replaced with that of the 320i to make it less inviting to car thieves. A wolf in sheep's clothing. 'To give you an advanced warning,' I said to Anji, 'entry is tight. They're going to pat you down.'

'For why?' she asked. 'Cheap thrills?'

'They had union trouble when they shut down the premises in the City and moved everything, including the print works, out here to this complex. They made a lot of staff redundant. That didn't go down well with the unions. There's a lot of people still holding a grudge. Hence, they're a bit paranoid about troublemakers and saboteurs.'

We pulled up at the barrier and were asked to get out of the car. Anji didn't look like a saboteur in her black knee-length skirt, white blouse buttoned up to the neck, pumps and false glasses. I stood ready to defuse any situation that might occur over an inappropriate shake-down, but it was me being paranoid. Again. I popped the boot of the Beamer and the guard had a good rummage around. Finally, we were allowed to progress.

Valentine was waiting in reception for us, not having our security passes yet. He looked as beautiful as the day before. He motioned us to some chairs and we sat down. At least I sat down. Anji stood there mesmerised. I introduced her and they shook hands. I wondered whether she would ever wash that hand again.

Valentine opened his briefcase and took out three lanyards and passes for the building. We put ours round our necks, and I put one in my pocket for Cherry.

'I've fixed you up with the CEO of the Gambling Division, Matthew Selby, as soon as we finish here. Then you see one of the three sisters before lunch . . .'

'One moment,' I said. 'The three sisters? Is that some kind of nickname?'

'Didn't my father tell you?'

'Tell me what?' I said, sensing bad news.

'That the three people who run the Casinos, Betting Shops and Online Betting are actually the three daughters of Campion?'

'Now, I wonder why he didn't tell me that before we signed the contract. Names please, and as much information as you have?' I turned to Anji. 'I think you should be taking notes.'

'Sorry,' she said. 'What did you say?'

'Take your notebook out and take notes.'

She shook her head as if forcefully clearing it. 'Ah, yes, notes,' she said, taking the notebook and a pen from her briefcase. Her hand was shaking.

'Carry on,' I said to Valentine.

'The three are called Violet, Rose and Petunia — sounds more like the Chelsea Flower Show than betting — respectively Head of Casinos, Betting Shops and Online Betting. I'd suggest you talk to Violet this afternoon, as I've allocated this evening to a visit to a casino — I'll pick you up at seven. That way we might be able to tick off Casinos today. Tomorrow I'll line up Rose and Petunia. Cool?'

'Cool,' said Anji. She got up from the chair. 'Excuse me, I just need a visit to the bathroom.'

'No probs,' said Valentine. He took out from his brief-case a one-inch thick wad of papers. He handed them to me. 'Everything you asked for is there. Accounts for the last three years, the last six months of updates on a rolling basis. I've arranged for you to have topmost access to the accounts — your ID and password is written down on the first sheet. I suggest you memorize them and then eat them.' He looked at me to see my reaction. I remained impassive. 'Joke,' he said.

'You're going to have to try harder,' I said.

Anji rejoined us, playing with fire. She had rolled over the top of her skirt so the hemline was now three inches above her knee and had undone the top two buttons of her blouse. The glasses were gone. I sensed a fatherly lecture from me brewing, otherwise we could have a complication to our plans.

We took the lift to the executive offices at the top of the building. The CEO of the Gambling Division, Matthew Selby, invited us to join him around a conference table in glass and chrome in a sizeable section of his office. Elsewhere were a desk and an informal meeting area of two sofas and a coffee table. He looked about forty, with flecks of grey in his dark hair. He was average height and slender and dressed in a conservative style that was guaranteed not to offend any-body. There was a sheaf of papers on the tabletop, which I gathered would be relevant at some stage during the course of the conversation. I was agog, though patient.

Before I sat down, I moved toward the window and, on the pretext of taking in the view, took a discreet look at his desk — you can tell a lot about someone from what was on their desktop. His had the standard computer terminal, a family photo of himself, wife and three young children, wife in designer clothes, and a copy of the *Guardian* opened to the crossword, three clues unsolved. What did that tell me? Liberal, intelligent, caring family man liking to remind himself of them throughout the day, short of creative spark maybe — apologies to *Guardian* readers — high-maintenance woman. Not much, but a good context in which to view him for the first time.

'Where would you like me to start?' he said.

'Some background on yourself,' I said, 'and then we'll move on to numbers.'

'Degree in English from Durham, where our family home was for the first twenty years of my life,' he said. 'I became a journalist for a local rag and gradually moved up the food chain via Fleet Street and then to here. Started out at the Publishing arm and got about as far as I could in what was a very competitive dog-eat-dog environment. I had started as a racing journalist, so had detailed knowledge of betting. This job came up — fresh start. Promotion. Great salary. Too big an opportunity to turn down. Three years on now.'

'Ever look back and have any regrets?' I asked.

'About as many as we all do. Only natural. If the chance of moving back to Publishing came up, I would take it, but it would have to be at CEO level. I'm not going to regress.'

'Tell me now about the casinos,' I said. 'Mr Shapiro said that results were mixed.'

'Overall, one would expect revenue to go down in the current economic times, and that is the picture outside the south-east.' He slid papers across the table to the three of us. 'Revenues are down four per cent, and that hits the bottom line big-time.'

I looked at the spreadsheet he had given me. 'But the picture is different elsewhere,' I said. 'Increases in the south-east, bucking the trend. Explanations?'

'None. But why should we worry? The profit shortfall and the increase almost balance themselves out. I don't see it warrants putting the casinos under the microscope. Things will return to normal when the current economic climate improves.'

I decided to shake the tree and see what fell on to the ground. This was not the time for subtlety.

'What will be Sir Gerald's likely course of action, if he wants to sell the Betting Division or the loss-making parts of it? Will Casinos be sacrificed for the current — or bad, one might say — position, or will he just find a buyer for Online Betting and the shops? Cut his losses.'

'I don't feel threatened, if that's what you are getting at. If the whole Betting Division is sold, the buyer will need to have someone running it. Continuity is on my side. Whether I would want to take that role is another matter. I'd love to get back to Publishing, though. Maybe I could just transfer across.'

'How about Online, next? What's the latest picture on that?'

'Hit by the economy, plus we have the new rules to try to get rid of gambling addiction — tighter regulations on lowering betting stakes being one of them. Overall, revenue down again and profits hit. But it's still the most important sector within the Gambling Division, and will increase with time. Profit margins down and lower than one might expect. The ratio of profit to revenue has decreased — something is wrong there.'

'What's your target margin?' I said.

'Slim, because of its size. Low margins, big numbers. We'd settle for just four per cent, but we've been way off target for the last six months. I can see why Sir Gerald is getting jittery.'

'Lastly, the betting shops?' I said. 'What's the position there?'

'Mixed,' he said. 'Similar position to Casinos. Volume up in the south and down elsewhere. No explanation. One would expect some revenue decrease because of business moving to virtual means. The old stigma of Betting Shops doesn't seem to go away: still an illicit image about it, raiding the biscuit barrel and blowing the housekeeping money — that sort of thing. I think the day of the betting shop is hanging on a thread. It's on borrowed time.'

'So, do you think Sir Gerald is right about selling the Gambling Division? Is it a shrewd business decision, or has he just lost courage about turning it around?'

He paused. 'No comment. Now I must get on.'

'Thank you for time,' I said. 'By the way, twelve across is *access*, sounds like *axes*. Quite appropriate, really: under the axe.'

* * *

I was caffeine deprived and getting twitchy. We had a window before the afternoon appointment with Violet. Time to put it to good use. 'Right, Valentine,' I said. 'Lead us to the coffee house.'

It was a mile walk and took us around twenty minutes before civilization appeared. The coffee shop was an independent business rather than part of a chain. The calm ambience was created by subtle lighting — no glaring or flickering fluorescent strips. Warm, friendly. I liked it instantly: long may it survive in the David and Goliath battle.

Although not large, there was room for about a dozen tables. I guessed that most of the customers were for takeaways from the Zeus complex. I grabbed a table and sent Valentine off for our order: Anji accompanied him. Big surprise!

A couple of minutes later, Valentine placed the coffees on the table and went off in search of the toilets. Good timing.

'Can you get your act together, Anji?' I said. 'Stop swooning and acting like a lovesick teenager.'

'Sorry, Nick,' she said, 'but isn't he gorgeous?'

'Play hard to get,' I said. 'Don't lose your self-respect.'

Valentine came back and took his seat. Anji made a poor attempt not to stare.

'OK, guys,' I said. 'What did we learn from that? You first, Anji. Tell me about Selby.'

'Square peg in a round hole,' she said. 'He should never have left Publishing.'

'Brilliant,' I said. 'This is sounding promising. Get your phones out. Google the Peter Principle. Your turn now, Valentine. Tell me about it?'

He looked at his phone — I was ashamed at the speed of his tapping. He nodded his head. 'In any hierarchy people rise to a level of respective incompetence. Always over-promoted.'

'Good,' I said. 'Now we're getting somewhere. It could be that the answer to the problems is simply to change the leader. Selby didn't know what was going on: maybe a fresh face is all that is needed. What else?'

'He talked about the economic climate,' said Anji. 'Blamed that for the decline in revenue and, hence, profit.'

'So why the erratic performance?' I said. 'Why are some areas for the betting shops and casinos bucking the trend? I don't buy that it is all down to a south-east effect. I would have felt northerners were traditionally the heaviest gamblers. No offence.'

'What is it, then?' Valentine said, leaning forward in anticipation of the words of wisdom.

'I don't have a clue,' I said.

They both sat back in their chairs, locked eyes and groaned.

'Maybe another coffee will help,' I said.

'My turn,' Anji said.

She got up and I laid a hand on Valentine's so that we had a moment of time together.

He recoiled. 'I'm not that way . . .'

'Nor me,' I said, removing my hand. 'I was thinking of girlfriends. How's your love life?' I said.

'Is that relevant?' he answered.

'Not to you, I suppose, but it is for me. Cut me some slack. Tell me about it?'

'Yet to find the right one,' he said. 'Had lots of first dates, but they're all so shallow. Hardly say a word. Maybe my technique is wrong. I'm still hopeful.'

'You could do worse than to try Anji,' I said.

'That would be brilliant,' he said, 'but I would have thought she must have a steady boyfriend.'

'Sometimes,' I said, 'playing it too cool doesn't work.'

Anji returned and dished out the coffees. 'Now what have you boys been talking about? Football? Cricket?'

'You missed out golfing and yachting,' I said. 'That's all you get for men: think of the grandpa aisle at Clintons.

Actually, though, we were talking about tonight. Valentine will pick you, me and Cherry up at seven o'clock. Dress code, Valentine?'

'Smart but casual,' he said.

'I've never really understood smart but casual,' I said. 'Would a bomber jacket and chinos do?'

'For tonight,' he said, 'but if you were to try our flagship casinos in London, Manchester or Leeds, for example, then that would be suits and ties. Night out with the missus. Birthday, anniversary, whatever. Make it special.'

'That's what I intend to do,' I said. 'Oh, yes. That's what I intend to do.'

'May I ask a question?' said Valentine.

'Fire away.'

'It seems to me,' he said, 'that you go out of the way to antagonise people. Why is that?'

'I'm a firm believer that the truth will out — the Home Secretary's unmasking is an example of that. Took fifteen years, but the truth did eventually come out. If I get people into offensive mode, they can't be defensive. They lower their guard. That's when I go in for the kill.' I formed a gun with my right hand, index finger pointed forward. Pulled the imaginary trigger. 'Bam.'

* * *

We headed back to the executive floor and waited for entry into Violet's domain. I had told Valentine to take notes, too, as well as Anji. I didn't want either of them to interrupt what I hoped to be a revealing interview. I wanted them to be in the background: a too-visible Shapiro's son might be overly intimidating.

Violet's room had the same layout as did Selby's, but slightly smaller. Desk area, informal seating with two settees and coffee table, conference table. The room was painted in terracotta and there was modern art on the walls. Geometric blocks of colour, wilting clocks, that sort of thing. She stood up from the desk — must remember to take a peek later — and extended her hand.

I didn't know yet whether she favoured her mother, but there were little of Campion's features in her face or build. She was tall and slim. Her hair was brown with progressive blonde highlights. If I had to guess her age — there's so many difficulties nowadays in the realm of cosmetic surgery — I would put it at mid-thirties. The most startling feature of her face were her eyes. Her blue eyes were accentuated by electric-blue eye shadow, prominent black lashes, eye liner and defining mascara. You were drawn into those eyes. Perhaps that was the intent: if you were drawn into her eyes, she was able to focus on yours.

She was looking like a stereotype of the powerful businesswoman in a tailored skirt suit, with the hem two inches above her knees, in a pale blue check pattern with a dark blue blouse and some three-inch nude heels — not confident enough to go for stilettos? There was a gold wedding ring and a long gold chain with a small heart-shaped medallion. Was there something significant there? A declaration of unending love? A permanent sign of her love or a reminder to her husband not to stray? Interesting.

We introduced ourselves and sat, as beckoned, at the table. 'I like the prints,' I said, to get the atmosphere off on the right foot. 'Have you always liked abstract art?'

'Since a teenager,' she said. 'I liked the thrill of the unpredictable. Saying something in a different way. A good maxim for life, don't you think?'

'I was wondering,' I said, 'whether you felt that being a daughter of Sir Gerald was a help or not?'

'You don't pull any punches do you, Shannon?' she said. 'Straight to the point.'

'We had to get there some time or another,' I said. 'Might as well get it out of the way.'

'I might ask the same question of Valentine here. What would be his answer?'

I nodded to Valentine so that he felt he could enter proceedings with my blessing.

'It's a bit of both,' he said. 'Without my father's power and authority behind me, I wouldn't have got the job — there are plenty of candidates out there with better CVs than mine, better degrees than my second class in Sociology from Warwick. Therefore, help. But others are guarded around me. I suspect I will never be treated as an individual in my own right. I'm a threat because of the connection. Stool pigeon territory. Enmity and envy from my being fast-tracked. Any day, I could be their boss.'

'You're perceptive, Valentine,' Violet said. 'That will stand you in good stead on your journey up the ladder, as you eventually will. As for me, the situation is more difficult because of being one of three daughters. The triumvirate, like in ancient Rome.'

'As far as my knowledge goes,' I said, 'neither of the triumvirates worked out well.'

'This time it will be different,' she said. 'Three divisions, three of us. It is destiny that we three will rule. We're nearly there.'

'How long have you been in charge of Casinos?' I asked. 'How long under Selby?'

'Current position, just under a year. Most of what we will talk about will be from that short period of time. As for Selby, he is a fish out of water. It won't be long before he makes a slip. Then the Division will be mine.'

'Selby admits that he can't explain the differential performance of north and south. Do you have any ideas?'

'Maybe it's because the south is more affluent and the north more guarded with their money.'

'All flat caps and ferrets? If that was the case,' I said, 'why hasn't that been reflected in the figures for past years? Why only now has it become more marked?'

She shrugged her shoulders dismissively. 'Whatever the explanation, there are casino managers out there who should be worried about their future. Might a breath of fresh air do some good?'

'I think that might be regarded as a case of *don't shoot the messenger*,' I said.

'You're too soft, Shannon,' she said. 'That might be your downfall.'

'It's been said many times. I'm like a cat — I have nine lives.'

'And how many have you got left?'

'One,' I said.

'I rest my case,' she said.

'Back to Casinos,' I said. It was me on the defensive now. Time to return to the plan. 'What about other factors? Have the ones in the south just been refurbished, say, and the ones in the north not so? It's often little things that turn out to be the drivers of change. We had a case a little while ago for a cinema chain. One city was losing money — audiences were heavily down. We didn't find a fraud. Instead, we found that the local bus company had brought forward the time of their last bus by half an hour. People would either have to leave and miss the last thirty minutes of the film or stay and get a cab.'

'Interesting case study,' Violet said, 'but I don't think it's relevant to us. We looked at all the extraneous factors and nothing showed up as an explanation.'

I remained impassive. Raised an eyebrow for good measure.

'Look,' Violet said. 'I have a master's degree in law. Law is all about detail. Remembering a whole host of cases and then sorting out the wheat from the chaff. If there was something going on, I would have spotted it.'

'Interesting,' I said. 'What university?'

'York,' she said. 'Not some tinpot place specialising in media studies. And what the hell has that got to do with it?'

'York's a long way from here. Hell of a drive. It's like putting a lot of distance between you and home. Should I read something into that?'

'The point of this meeting is about Casinos,' she said forcefully, 'not about some sort of characterisation. Get on with it, Shannon.'

I gave a cry of pain. 'Excuse me for a moment. I need to stretch my leg. Old wound from childhood.'

I stood up, marched up and down by the table, headed for the window, turned around so I could see her desk. There was a picture of Violet with what I assumed to be her two sisters and mother. No Campion. What should I read into that? Maybe something like not wanting to spoil the picture by including Campion's florid face.

There were also manila folders of papers neatly stacked in piles — in, out, urgent? — I couldn't see from this distance. Showed a methodical mind deriving from her legal training. Maybe she was right in her nose not sniffing anything wrong from going through the data on the casinos. The computer screen showed she was working on a spreadsheet: again, I couldn't see what it related to. A desk drawer was partly open. Inside I could see a packet of Silk Cut and a gold Dunhill lighter. Good taste on the lighter, bad that she was a smoker. I wondered how many times a day she had to make the trip downstairs for a crafty fag and how easy it would be for someone to pop into her office and have an even craftier peek at the folders?

'Sorry about that,' I said, walking back to the table and sitting back down.

'Don't get yourself comfortable,' Violet said. 'This interview is over for now.'

For now? What did she mean by that? So many questions, so few answers.

'Thank you for your time,' I said. 'Much appreciated when you must have so many more pressing matters.'

We gathered our papers, shook hands again and left her in peace. I thought I detected a sigh of relief from her.

Exit stage left.

* * *

31

Returning to our allocated small office, I realized that we needed more space to lay out the volumes of data we had been given. 'Time to head back and make a start of trying to unravel the information,' I said. 'Sorry to leave you, Valentine, but we'll see you later when you pick us up.'

'Valentine could come back with us,' Anji said, 'so that he doesn't miss out on anything. You said he needs to learn from this exercise, see what we do and how we go about it.'

I doubted she would retain attention if she was away from Valentine and stressing about what he might get up to. She was going to stick with him like glue; there didn't seem to be any harm in it.

'Tally ho!' I said.

'Tally ho?' said Valentine.

'It's what the riders say to kick start the fox chase,' I said.

'So last century,' said Anji.

Thanks for being supportive, Anji, I thought.

'Cool,' said Valentine.

'Yeah, cool,' said Anji.

If it carries on like this, I'm going to need an interpreter. Not yet forty and I feel like a dinosaur. Still, tally ho.

CHAPTER FIVE

I got Anji to ring Morag and warn her that we had a client — albeit a very junior one — coming back with us, so that she could hide away any sensitive papers. Valentine loved the ride in the Beamer and declared it was even more fun than the open-top Beetle his father had bought him for his twenty-first birthday. He was wowed by our building and Anji couldn't wait to show him around. She insisted he should stay with us till the car came at seven to take us to the casino.

I set all the papers onto the conference table and sorted them into the three sectors of the Gambling Division — Online, Betting Shops and Casinos — Casinos being the top priority for now. We could start off with the data on that, so that we would be familiarised before our trip to Lakeside. Beryl made us some proper coffee and we assembled around the table.

'Spreadsheets,' I said to Anji. 'Construct one with the revenue and profits for the last twelve months by location and break them down against performance in the previous year. See if there are any patterns. We'll work from there through other parameters.'

'Valentine can read the figures to me while I type,' Anji said.

That meant they had to sit close together. Shame!

'Fire,' said Valentine.

'Fire,' Anji echoed.

'Where?' I said.

'Not real fire,' Anji said. 'It means something good.'

'Then why did you have to say it in terms I couldn't understand?' I asked.

'To give you the first lesson in how us guys speak nowadays,' Anji said. 'We've got to get you up to speed in case you ever want to speak with young people. You never know — our next job might be for a young, trendy company.'

I sighed, not relishing my next tutorial, and left them to get on with it while I sat with Norman and Cherry in the river room overlooking the Thames. I needed to think things through and they would be a perfect sounding board.

'The premise of this job,' I said to them, 'was that the fall in profits was down to some sort of fraud or frauds. It's early days, and only one sector is being investigated so far, but I'm wondering whether it might just be down to bad management. Selby, the Head of the Division, doesn't seem to have a clue about what's going on.'

'How long ago did this hit on profits start?' said Cherry.

'Just looking at Casinos — we've yet to get on to Online and Betting Shops, goodness knows what the pictures are like there — it began about eight months ago after the last audit. But the strange thing is the differential between north and south.'

'Any cash involved?' asked Norman, always straight to the point. 'You do know how much I like cash.'

'I wouldn't have thought so: everyone uses credit or debit cards nowadays.'

'See what happens when you get to the Betting Shops' arm of the Division,' he said. 'Cash is the way to hide money from the missus, and that's what addicts do.'

'My suspicions, too,' I said.

'I must go and get changed,' said Cherry. 'Am I still with you tomorrow?'

'Would be good,' I said. 'No one's responding to me shaking the tree so far. Different approach might help.'

'See you in an hour,' she said. 'Shall I tell Anji and Valentine — what an intriguing name — to pack up so Anji can get changed, and send Valentine in here?'

'Sounds like a plan,' I said. 'I suspect Anji will want a lot of time to get ready for tonight. I'm feeling a little black dress in the air.'

Cherry left and a couple of minutes later Valentine came into the room.

'Time for a snifter, Valentine?' said Norman. 'We've got most things.'

'Do you have any cider?' he asked.

'When I said we've got most things,' Norman said, 'that didn't include cider. Try a vodka instead. Orange juice or tonic?'

'Any coke?' he said. Norman nodded. 'Maybe that and some rum?'

'Attaboy,' said Norman. 'We have white rum, golden from the Caribbean, and old-fashioned spiced dark rum.'

'I'll try the golden, please,' he said. 'Never had that before.'

'That's the attitude,' Norman said. 'Try something new. Expand your repertoire. Good lesson for life.'

'If you fix drinks — I'll go for my usual,' I said, '—I'll go and get changed. Won't take me a minute.'

'Right,' said Norman. 'Come and sit down, Valentine. Enjoy a drink and watch the sun going down over the river. Chill.'

I left them to it. I hoped Norman wouldn't pour his usual generous measure. We needed Valentine sober enough to be our guide at the casino and pull any strings if needed.

Five minutes later, dressed in my favourite suede bomber jacket, black T-shirt and sand chinos, feeling as cool as the ice in my vodka, I rejoined them. Valentine looked relaxed. Why not? Soon to have a beautiful young girl at his side and a fun evening ahead. I noticed that more than half of his drink had gone.

'Bathroom?' he said.

'Through the door, across the hall and it's straight ahead,' I said. He set off, following the directions. When he had left, Norman said to me, 'God, he's green, Nick. If you were planning to use him for the investigation, I wouldn't count on it.'

'He only graduated six months ago,' I said in his defence, 'and I suspect, because of his patronage, that he wouldn't have got much help since then. I don't think his father did him any favours bringing him into the business. Just aroused feelings of distrust among those who should have been training him. They can't wait to see him fail.'

'Fresh-faced, young and innocent,' Norman said. 'He needs a mentor. The bad news is, that might be you.'

Valentine came back in the room followed by Cherry and Anji. They looked stunning. Anji had on a short little black dress with a halter neck that showed off her shoulders to best effect. She had on a pair of impossibly high heels. Her hair sparkled and smelt like almonds, her make-up subdued for whatever the bright lights would throw down on her. Valentine took an intake of breath.

Cherry was wearing a black dress, low cut with no straps and those long gloves that ended in line with the top of the dress. She had pinned up her hair and secured it with combs. Her heels were high — but not as high as Anji's. As I said, they both were stunning; it bears repeating. I was feeling underdressed as someone to accompany two such women.

There was the toot of a horn outside. Our car had arrived. Hold the roulette wheel.

* * *

The car turned out to be a Range Rover from Campion's fleet and had plenty of room for all of us to sit in comfort on the journey. I imagined Anji was disappointed. The casino was an adjunct of the retail area and next to a multiplex cinema and bowling alley. There were plenty of restaurants, all generic brands that you would find in any main town, that

36

were doing a roaring trade when we arrived at eight o'clock. A man in a black suit greeted us, took our names and car registration so that we wouldn't be charged for going over the permitted time of two hours and pointed us to the action.

The place was quiet. Maybe we were too early — eight o'clock and before the post-dinner trade arrived. Things would hot up later, surely — this was supposed to be where profits were up.

There were the ever-present slot machines at the front, already with punters piling coins into them and one player feeding two machines simultaneously, and three tables that I could see: blackjack, roulette and baccarat. In one corner of the room, there was a bar and seating area. In another, there was a restaurant with typical old-fashioned pub food — steaks, battered fish, things in a basket. Overhead there was subdued lighting that gave the room a warm glow and accentuated the beauty of Cherry and Anji, causing a stir.

There was a caged area with two cashiers that took cash or card payments. I stood behind another man in a short queue. When I got to the front to buy chips, I looked to my left where a middle-aged portly man with a shaved head produced a huge pile of cash. The man behind him looked put out that the cash had to be counted and verified, cutting into his game time. Counting complete, the cashier said, 'Ten thousand, sir. As usual for the chips, Mister Simpson?'

'Man of habit,' he said.

Ten thousand was a hell of a lot to venture. I paid by card for chips in tens of one thousand pounds — four hundred for me, two hundred each to Cherry, Anji and Valentine. All going on expenses if we lost!

A waiter carrying a tray came next to him. He handed the drink to Simpson. 'With our compliments, sir.'

'Good luck,' I said to Simpson. 'All us gamblers should stick together.'

'And good luck to you,' he said.

I told the waiter to come over to where our group was standing to take our drinks order — not complimentary for us non high rollers. I saw Simpson head to the blackjack table and was curious about him. Ten grand was a lot of cash.

'Valentine,' I said, 'the guy over there is called Simpson. I want you to find out all about him. Pull rank and get everything.'

Our drinks arrived just as Valentine came back and handed me a single sheet of A4. I put it in my jacket pocket to study later. We sat down to plan strategy. Time for a quick tutorial. 'First lesson: only bet what you can afford to lose. Set a limit and stick to it. Second lesson: the odds are stacked in favour of the casino, which is the margin it makes. Your best chance is roulette, where the margin in the casino's favour is three per cent, more if the wheel has two zeros rather than the standard one. Third lesson: if playing blackjack the margin is around six per cent, can be up to twenty-one per cent according to what card you and the dealer are dealt first and your game strategy — when to draw and when to stand.'

'Blackjack?' Anji said. 'Tell me more.'

'It's a variant of what we British call pontoon. It's called different names dependent on where you come from. The American name is more used rather than the French vingt-et-un. It's whoever comes closest to twenty-one without going bust, which is going over twenty-one. Baccarat is pretty much the same as blackjack except that the target is nine rather than twenty-one — it's the favourite game of James Bond. As for me, I'm off to blackjack. Take your pick, but you'll probably do best to stick to roulette. You'll still lose, but your money will last longer. And, Valentine, that's your last drink. Don't blame me. I'm only doing what your father would do in these circumstances. Tonight, you're on duty. You're my responsibility. OK? Don't let me down.'

'I'll look after him,' said Anji.

'I'll come with you,' said Cherry. 'Someone has to stop you being smug.'

Simpson was already playing when we arrived at the table. All seats were taken, so we stood behind him. I caught the dealer's eye. 'Kibitz,' I said to her, meaning I would watch and bet on the hands of one of the players.

'Do you mind?' I said to Simpson?

'Be my guest,' he said.

The croupier started to deal out the cards. Simpson's first card was a ten — a very good card since a king, queen, jack or ten would give him a count of twenty, as close as you could get to twenty-one, and an ace would give him twenty-one exactly. He put a fifty-pound chip on the table. I put down three ten-pound chips.

Simpson's second card was a six. When the dealer has a count of sixteen or below, he or she is required to draw another card — it's a good practice to follow. Simpson chose to stand, not taking another card. The dealer's count was fifteen. He was forced to draw another card — it was a king and went bust. We had the winning bet and the dealer had to pay out.

There are two types of gamblers: the professional who knows the odds and adopts best possible strategy of when to stand — not taking a third or more card — and the amateur player who just likes the thrill of it all and who rides on adrenaline. Simpson was from the latter group. From the bets he placed, I could tell that he had no knowledge of the odds of winning or losing. I doubted whether he really cared about the outcome as long as he could keep playing, feeling that buzz.

My four-hundred pile of chips was soon down to three-forty.

'Time to cash up,' Simpson said, exercising some restraint at last.

'Let me buy you a drink before you go,' I said. 'Unwind.'

'I'll get you one instead,' he said. I noticed he didn't say *buy*, but *get*. Compliments of the house again, I presumed.

We went to the bar area and found a quiet table. I introduced Cherry and myself and he summoned the barman, keeping one eye on Cherry.

'You light up the room,' he said to her.

'Thank you, kind sir,' she replied in the voice of a Victorian housemaid.

'Only telling the truth,' said Simpson.

While he was talking to the waiter, I had the chance to study him in more detail. He was short and, putting it politely, bulgy. His suit jacket, though, was loose on him, meaning that he must have lost weight recently. His face had a double chin and was marred by a scar running from under his left eye to his mouth. Some serious injury in the past to go that far, I would think. Probably not a Heidelberg duelling scar — those days are long gone. He was completely bald, and I would think he had shaved his head recently. His eyes were brown, and all the time he was talking to Cherry they were darting around as if he was keeping watch for some threat.

'Are you a regular?' Cherry said to him.

'I come here Monday to Friday at eight o'clock. Spend ninety minutes playing blackjack and then go out for a meal — if I had to criticize this place, it would be that the food here is terrible. I prefer gourmet fare rather than chicken in a basket.'

'The important question,' I said, 'for any gambler, is "are you lucky?"'

'Moderately,' he said. 'Well, no actually, now I come to think of it. Still, it's all good clean fun. Fine way to spend an evening, especially when meeting new friends like you. Tell me what you do?'

'We're just humble accountants out with two staff for a bonding session,' Cherry said. 'That's what our consultant said. Be closer together. Build team spirit.'

'How about you?' I said. 'What do you do? Do you need a good accountant?'

'My business can be best described as import/export,' he said.

Well, that was informative. Could be anything.

'Nothing interesting,' he said. 'I'm well looked after as far as an accountant goes, but I'll keep you in mind if ever I need someone new.' He fished in the top pocket of his jacket and brought out a business card and gave it Cherry. 'Here's my details. Send me a brochure.'

'Most gamblers are superstitious,' she said, following the mantra of keep him talking if you want to learn things. 'How about you? Any lucky charms or special rituals you go through? You know, right-foot sock always on before the left, saluting a magpie. Black cats and so on?'

'I always put on the same tie as you see now. Colours of my old school. Silly sentimental thing to do.'

Didn't seem to be working, on the evidence of this evening.

'Blackjack is a tricky game,' I said, 'the odds change after every card is dealt. There are 1326 permutations of any two cards. To win at blackjack you need to know the odds of each point count between two and twenty-one compared with the dealer's hand as revealed by the dealer's face up card.'

'Excuse my friend,' Cherry said. 'He should get out more.'

He finished his gin and tonic and stood up. 'Must fly,' he said. 'My driver will be waiting, and there's a dim sum calling.' He shook our hands and started to walk away. He turned to take one last look at Cherry. 'Stunning,' he said. 'I hope to see you again.'

We watched him make his way to the cashiers' booths with his reduced pile of chips.

'What do you make of that?' Cherry said.

'Got good taste,' I said. 'Edgy, though — the way his eyes are darting around all the time.'

'Do you think he's lonely?' she said. 'Coming here five times a week on his own?'

'Lousy blackjack player, for one thing that's certain. Must be rolling in it. On top of his losses, there's the cost of a gourmet meal and a driver. They treat him like a lord here. Must make him feel important. I wonder what he imports and exports. Tat from China? Fake watches? Whatever it is, he didn't want to elucidate. Something he felt ashamed of? Sex toys? At least we know where to find him for the future.'

'Let's go and find Anji and Valentine,' she said. 'See how they're doing and what mischief they're in.'

'In a moment. I want to talk about Valentine. What's your view of him? Anji is certainly smitten. Norman said Valentine was green and had much to learn. He has no arrogance, and I doubt he knows how attractive he is. Doesn't lord it over people by using his position. I'm getting to kind of liking him. Where do you stand?'

'He is certainly beautiful. I can understand why Anji goes weak at the knees whenever she's near him. In terms of looks, he is pretty much perfect: if there's a flaw, I can't find one. After that, I agree with Norman. Valentine has so much to learn, and nobody is teaching him anything. He's like a blank canvas waiting for the artist to start painting. But, all things considered, he's a nice guy. As a woman, I want to scoop him up and hug him tightly, protect him from the world. He deserves better than what he's got at the moment. His career will fail at only the first step up the ladder. I feel for him.'

'Me, too,' I said. 'Maybe we can get him on the right path, teach him some basics, while we're on the job. OK. Let's go and see how they have done.'

We finished the last of our drinks and walked over to the roulette table. There was a fine-looking croupier — a smartly-dressed woman in black with her blonde hair out of the way in a plait — and the pit boss — the person charged with making sure everything was done perfectly and there was no cheating. Anji and Valentine were engrossed in the action of the wheel and didn't notice us immediately. There were no chips in front of Anji: Valentine, in contrast, had a huge stack.

'Look at this,' Anji said, pointing to Valentine's pile. 'He can't go wrong. Red has come up six times in a row and he's left his bet there each time, doubling up. Must be . . .'

'Thirty-two,' I said. 'If it was a ten-pound bet at first, he will be three hundred and twenty pounds up. Time to quit. We've had our fun for the evening.'

We left the table just as black came up. Phew! Good to have Lady Luck on your side. We cashed up, the cashier offering us the option to take it in cash or straight into a bank account, and walked to the door where our driver, presumably bored out of his skull, was chatting to the doorman.

We walked towards the car. A blue van was blocking it. A man stood there with an axe. Not a hand axe, but a real Gimli-style axe, a proper lumberjack's axe. The windscreen of our car was shattered. A thick-set man stared at us and turned towards the van, weighing up the possible courses of action — make a quick exit, if that was now possible, or face us down. The power in his axe made up his mind. He decided to try to scare us off.

'Anji!' I shouted. 'Take off your shoes. Make a run for it. Get Valentine inside and get Security to call the police.'

'Can you take the rear?' I said to Walker.

'I got it, Shannon,' she said.

I tossed her one of Anji's shoes and picked up the other. We were armed with our version of stilettos. Better than nothing.

The man raised the axe and turned to face me, ignoring any threat that Walker posed. I wasn't going to give him any thinking time. I advanced on him, waving the shoe. He laughed. As well he might.

He swung the axe. Should have chosen a smaller weapon. It was too heavy, even for a man of his bulk. There was a moment for each swing where the axe carried through too far and needed more time before swinging back. I pulled the stiletto back, ready for a chance to get through his defences. As the axe got to the farthest point in its trajectory. I leapt in and hit his axe hand, driving the point of the shoe home.

He let out a cry of pain. The shoe was now stuck firmly in his hand. He didn't know what to do — he needed both hands to get the shoe out and couldn't let go of his only weapon. It would have been laughable given other circumstances.

The van voted for saving the driver's skin rather than his accomplice and roared away.

The man with the axe placed his feet wide for maximum balance. He was focused on me, his need for revenge, for survival even, clouding his mind. That was when Walker struck. She kicked him from behind in his groin, bringing forth another cry of pain. He doubled up. I hit him with a straight left to the stomach. His body didn't know what to do: the kick from Walker driving him one way and the punch in the stomach the other. Walker gave him another kick and he collapsed on the ground. I kicked the axe away and stood over him. Saved by a shoe!

The Security man — with none of the skills of a bouncer — arrived on the scene just as the action was over.

'Time to hand over to you,' I said. 'You've called the police?'

'Be here any minute,' he said. 'Impressive.'

'We'll be inside,' I said. 'Nice work, Walker.'

'Thanks, Shannon. You did well, too.'

The incident over, it was back to Cherry again. We walked back to the door and found Anji and Valentine. His face was ashen. His stare unwavering. He couldn't process what had happened.

'We owe you a pair of shoes, Anji,' I said. 'Put it on expenses.'

'Is that all you have to say?' Valentine asked, trembling. 'You've just been attacked by a mad axeman, and all you can do is talk about a pair of shoes?'

'You'll get used to it,' said Anji. 'An everyday story of countryfolk. We haven't had any dead bodies yet. Bound to come sooner or later.'

'There's only one thing to add,' I said. 'Anyone fancy chicken in a basket?'

* * *

The police did what they could, which was little. They confiscated the axe and asked a lot of questions and got nothing in return. The axeman stood there clutching his groin and remaining silent, except for the regular groans of pain. The police said that he was probably waiting for a hotshot lawyer to turn up and get him off the hook, or, at least, to reduce any charges.

They didn't sound confident. How is it someone can threaten a person with an axe and not be decently punished? Just walk clear from a slap on the wrist from a magistrate who was having a good day?

Some things just don't make sense.

CHAPTER SIX

I awoke at five o'clock, after only two hours sleep courtesy of waiting to get a new windscreen with a backhander of a large wad of cash for unsocial hours, with the same question on my mind with which I had gone to sleep. Why us? It was too much of a coincidence for it to be a random attack. We were the target. We had given our names and our car registration to gain entry. The doorman must have relayed the information to the attackers, whoever they were. So the doorman must be in on it — maybe that explained the tardiness of his behaviour. But what was he into and who was paying him?

I remembered the note about Simpson and, tiptoeing across the room so as not to disturb Cherry, went to the wardrobe and fished it out of the pocket of my bomber jacket. I read the information. There was little there:

Thomas Simpson. Gold service — I presumed this was the reason why he got the free drinks. Bank account in the name of a company called Backswing. Sort code, account number. Address — somewhere in rural Essex that I had never visited, but probably classy, judging by the amounts he was betting. And that was it.

'What are you doing?' said Cherry, waking up. 'Have you seen the time, Shannon?'

'Couldn't sleep,' I said. 'Sorry to have woken you. I thought I'd just read the information on Simpson.'

'And what has it told you?' she said.

I told her the few details I now had.

'You know what's happening, don't you?' she said.

'I've been putting it off. If we're right, and I think you have come to the same conclusion as me, there's a whole new dimension to the job. It won't be only a windscreen that was hit by the axe. We've stumbled on something we shouldn't. What to do is the question?'

'Simpson is laundering money, isn't he?' she said.

I nodded.

'Deposit cash,' she said, 'chips remaining at the end of the evening credited to his bank account. A bit of jiggery pokery on the books and no one's the wiser.'

'Is Simpson the brains for the scheme,' I said, 'or is there someone else above him? Is he a criminal mastermind or foot soldier? If foot soldier, are there more Simpsons out there? So many questions, not enough answers.'

'We're going to need Arthur,' she said. 'Do some poking around and watch our back.'

'I'll set up a meeting with him before we have dinner with the Campions. I'll get the man from Abacus . . .'

'. . . "You can count on us". Such a brilliant strap line. Second only to "we specialise in everything".'

'We can get him to do some tracking on some of the people from Zeus,' I said. 'The three sisters and Selby for a start.'

'Come back to bed,' Cherry said. 'Things always look better in the morning.'

'And we've got a plan,' I said.

She patted the space next to her. 'And I've got a better one.'

* * *

Before we left for the Zeus complex, I briefed Anji.

'I know you have done this before,' I said, 'but Valentine is new to the game. Let's put him to another test. Tie up

47

with Norman and see what you can find out about this company. Make Valentine do as much of the work as possible.' I handed her Simpson's business card and the sheet of paper that Valentine had got from the casino. 'Simpson said his business was import/export,' I said, 'but his card says diamond dealer. Seems a strange thing to say.'

'Would he be worried about giving too much away and setting himself up for a mugging?' Anji said.

'Possible,' I said, 'but I keep thinking about all that cash every night. Maybe diamond dealers do a lot of their transactions in cash. I don't know. Do your best.'

The three of us set off in the Beamer to meet Valentine before our meeting with Petunia. Back in our small office it was getting overcrowded, never intended for four people at one time. I sat Cherry and Anji at the desk and Valentine and I wheeled in two spare chairs from the general office.

'I've been thinking,' Valentine said.

'Yes?' I said dubiously.

'Couldn't sleep,' he said, 'mind still whirring, overdose of adrenaline, I suppose. Maybe one more rum and coke than I should have had. Anyway, you know that old joke of the North starting at Watford? What if it's sort of true. I'd like to try something. Another variable on the spreadsheet.'

'Which is?' I said.

'Travel time from London,' he said.

'Brilliant thought, Valentine,' said Cherry.

Show more faith, Shannon, I rebuked myself. The boy could be a genius.

Anji called up the spreadsheet and inserted a new column. 'I'll handle inputs if you check the distances,' she said to Valentine. 'We can adjust the travelling times from there. It was your idea, after all. Google Maps could be our friend.'

Half an hour later, I heard a cheer from Valentine and Anji. 'Got it,' they said in unison. Cherry and I got up close to the spreadsheet and peered over their shoulders.

'What have you got?'

'All the casinos that have been doing well are within an hour or so's drive from London.'

'So,' said Cherry, 'unless Simpson has a helicopter, he isn't alone.'

'Looks like a well-organised team,' I said. 'This is money laundering on an industrial scale. Norman will say "I told you so". It's always down to the cash.'

* * *

Petunia's office, even though she was Head of Online Betting, wasn't, understandably, quite as spacious as Selby's. Not on a corner, so only the one window to look out on the empire. She welcomed us and shook our hands and then went to the conference table. We followed in her wake.

The first thing that I noticed about her was that she was too thin, almost bordering on the anorexic. I put her down as a worrier, since she otherwise looked healthy. Her hair was auburn and cut to shoulder length — looked more like random cutting rather than some sort of style. But what did I know? Could be the latest fashion craze.

Her eyes were brown and looked watchful. She was dressed in what I thought was a designer version of M&S, tailored grey jacket and matching skirt. Nice fit, shame about the colour. This was one dreary woman. Her make-up was low-key and her lips were a dull brown. As she placed her hands on the table, I saw the yellow stain of nicotine that comes with being a heavy smoker. This was a woman that lived on the edge of her nerves.

I introduced Anji, Cherry and myself: she knew Valentine and gave him a cursory glance to put him in his place. His level in the food chain didn't even warrant an acknowledgement. They both took out notepads and looked industrious.

'Profits in Online are down,' I said. 'It's our job to find out why. Any ideas?'

'If I did, then we wouldn't need you.'

'Excuse my colleague,' said Cherry, playing good cop to my bad cop. 'He is apt to be a bit blunt. When did you first notice something had changed?'

'We have always had a constant per cent of margin of profits. Around nine months ago, the margin went down.'

My god, I thought. *It took that long for the penny to drop.*

'It shouldn't happen — the computer algorithm sets the odds and should maintain the margin. Something has gone amiss. We're paying out more than we should.'

'Do you know whether it's more winning bets, or a higher than average payout?' I said. 'A loss, say, on a big race or football match?

'Payouts are limited,' she said. 'Back to the computer.'

'Surely an event like Leicester winning the League costs a lot,' Cherry said.

'The betting industry learned a lot from that. Systems have been tightened. You should read our terms and conditions. The punter can back something at 100/1, but we're protected. In the terms and conditions, there is a weasel that states there is a maximum payout.'

'And how much might that be?' said Cherry.

'Currently, one hundred thousand pounds,' said Petunia.

'Wow!' I said.

'We can lay some of the bet off with other bookmakers in smaller amounts, so as not to flag what was happening. Sooner or later, the competition will sniff something wrong and that avenue will close down. And there's also the option of cashing out for the punter. Paying out on a live bet for those who like the security of pounds in hand rather than the risk of losing everything. That option is usually more frequent with horse racing, but it happens in football, too. You might have an accumulator on six races where your first five selections have won, and the punter will take a payout rather than risk getting nothing if your sixth selection loses.'

'So,' Cherry said, 'are we looking at a few big bets, or a lot of small ones, or a combination of both?'

'What you have to bear in mind is that the computer logs each bet as it is laid and adjusts the odds to take account of it. The fraudster would have to make a lot of small bets laid at the very last minute to mean there's not a chance of the computer picking them up before the event starts.'

'I understand that the computer can be overridden by a human being — an expert in the field. Can that be the cause of the profit drop?' I said.

'Any adjustment would have to go through our watcher section — that's what we call the person who oversees the expert,' Petunia said dismissively. 'A second line of defence. And I know what you are going to say. What about collaboration between the expert and the watcher? Very little chance. All the experts and watchers are heavily vetted. They are not recruited to be team players. And, at the end of the day, there's always Selby.'

The blind leading the blind, I wondered.

'What about special events?' asked Cherry. 'Maybe something like Prince Charles abdicating within six months of inheriting the throne? Another example — there's a world chess championship coming up later this week. What odds would you set for that? Who would be your first line of defence? Presumably the algorithm would have nothing to compute, no past evidence to work from?'

'It's rare, but it would be calculated by one expert and run through a panel of experts. It would need a sizeable bet to make that worthwhile.'

'Are there any patterns around the losses — same expert, say?' I asked.

Petunia took a moment to answer. I thought she might try to bluff, for I didn't think she had tried looking at this. 'I don't think that is possible,' she said.

My suspicions confirmed.

'I'd like a list of all experts by expertise, and the same for the watchers,' I said. 'Plus any irregularities you have noticed. By size, by event, by anything else you can think of. Till then, we'll get out of your hair.'

* * *

'I must say,' said Cherry when we were back in our cubby hole, 'you handled that with your normal dose of diplomacy and tact.'

'You know my style,' I said, 'you've got to shake the tree and see what fruit falls to the ground.'

'And what have you got so far?'

'A banana, or rather a banana skin. This company is due for a skid. In around three years, it will all be run by the three daughters and continue its recent decline. I know we've yet to meet Rose, but I'm not impressed so far. It could well be that we've started to crack the casinos, but it was Valentine who came up with the idea, not Violet or Selby. The picture is forming; the corners of the jigsaw are falling into place.'

'And what's the picture on the box?'

'Everyone has been promoted beyond their capabilities. It needs a complete change of management style and competency. A clear out of those not able to pull their weight. It will be interesting to hear what Campion says over dinner. To see if he's aware of what's going on. What the future is going to look like.'

'I think it needs the subtlety of a woman's touch,' said Cherry. 'I'll take Petunia to lunch tomorrow.'

'Why stop there? Invite them all out. Kill three birds with one stone?'

'I'll give it a try,' she said.

'Good luck with that,' I said. 'See if you can convince Petunia to eat more than a single lettuce leaf.'

'She is a bit skeletal, I admit.'

'What are you going to say for them to agree to lunch?'

'No problem. They'll all be agog to find out what was said over dinner this evening. And more than a little curious about you. They will want to size up the enemy i.e., you. Good cop, bad cop again.'

'See if you can find out their background,' I said. What makes them tick? What's Petunia's long-term goal? I don't know what she wants next. She is in the smallest Division after Publishing and Broadcasting. She'll look for something bigger than that. That job won't satisfy her for long.'

'What will we do now? Cherry asked.

'Gather the evidence. Locate customers using the same method. Buy chips with cash, deposit chips into a bank account. It couldn't be easier. Theoretically.'

* * *

Rose Campion, although the twin sister of Petunia, was a different kettle of fish — whatever that means. She might be regarded as slightly overweight by those who make that judgement: size 14, 12 at a push if she lay on the bed to put her jeans on. Her hair was titian, had a Claudia Winkleman fringe and finished at a perfectly manicured shoulder length: not one hair out of place. She had brown eyes that clashed with her make-up, which was overdone and suggested that she was about to go clubbing with the girls. She was wearing a tight white top and a short skirt in black. There was a gold stud below her lips — that said it all.

'Who are these people?' she asked me, before I could make the formal introductions.

I introduced all of us. 'What is their function?' she said, pointing to Anji and Valentine.

'One of them is learning the job,' I said. 'I haven't decided which yet.' I thought, I hoped, it was going to confuse her — shake that tree, Shannon.

She consulted her sports watch, for what would become a habit during our meeting, and sighed. 'What do you want to know?' she said.

'Tell me, any trends this year?' I said. 'Turnover, profits and anything else that might be relevant. Before that, a bit of context would be good. Tell me your history?'

Most people love to talk about themselves. It's a good way to start a dialogue.

'Educated at private school and then Politics at Cambridge. I've been here ten years. Too long only to be finishing with control of Betting Shops.'

'What would you rather have?' said Cherry. 'Either here or somewhere else.'

53

'No question about it,' she said. 'Head of Broadcasting. I need to stretch my wings.'

'Wouldn't that be on the table for your sisters? Would that not be stepping on their toes?'

'Rest assured,' she said, 'everyone will get what they want. The plan is set.'

'So, the second part of the question,' Cherry said. 'The betting shops. Can you give us some details?'

'The shops are a dead man walking. No, the rising of the dead man walking. More and more, the punters are moving Online. Very soon, they will be closed. The saving grace is that it gives Zeus a presence in the high street. Helps keep the brand in the punters' minds. We'll tolerate them for a while longer, but that's only postponing the inevitable.'

'Latest trends?' I said.

'As you might expect, the trend is downwards. The south less so. The north down by about ten per cent, the south only by two per cent. It's a self-fulfilling prophecy. The shops have terminals for punters to access their online accounts. Why do they need that? They could access easier at home or in the office. Most people nowadays — certainly our customers — have access to a computer and Wi-Fi. My guess is that it is a social thing. They come to meet others like themselves, maybe socialise their guilt. Oh, what a tangled web we weave.'

'I noticed,' I said, 'that everyone we've spoken to talks about punters — not customer or clients or even, that horrible euphemism, stakeholders. It doesn't seem to hold much respect.'

'You're joking, surely. What sort of business do you have? Whatever it is, it won't be viable: unless you change it will go under. We respect their money. That's all you need to know.'

She laughed and shook her head. I felt like doing the same.

'Anji,' I said, 'give Ms Campion the list of what we need.'

I watched Anji take the papers from her briefcase and walk the long way across the room. She stopped at the desk to support herself as she fixed something with her shoe. Satisfied, she handed the papers to Rose. I looked at the pair of them. Anji was dressed older than Rose. The stud under Rose's lips gleamed in the light. I rest my case.

* * *

We three — Cherry, Anji and I — travelled back to our office, leaving Valentine to scour through the HR records of some key personnel. In the car, talk was focused on our interviews, with Rose being the main topic of conversation.

'What did you see on her desk?' I said to Anji. 'Nice trick with the shoe, by the way. You're learning so much, so quickly.'

'Thank you,' she said. 'There was an iPad with a graph on it. From what I could see, I think the graph seemed to be keeping track of her weight. She wants to drop a size or two. She should talk to Petunia and get some tips from the horse's mouth. The desk was empty apart from the laptop computer.'

'So, what did you make of Rose, Anji?' Cherry asked.

'Rearrange the words lamb and mutton,' she said. 'I'd say she is self-obsessed. I wouldn't be surprised if she hadn't had the skills of the most experienced cosmetic surgeon — brow a bit too rigid to be natural, breasts too big, liposuction, maybe. Probably got some tattoos hidden away, only to be revealed in intimate moments.'

'Am I getting the wee vibe that you don't like her very much,' I said.

'I've seen her type before,' she said, 'on the circuit.' By which she meant the pole-dancing circuit. 'Fear of getting old — usually forty is the crisis level where they can fall off the cliff edge — and the desperate search for eternal youth. It can cause them to make dangerous decisions, usually getting involved with the wrong sort of man or a series of wrong men. Abuse can be common. Not a place to be.'

'Well said,' Cherry said. 'A brilliant bit of characterization.'

'Or character assassination,' I said.

'You did ask for my opinion.' Anji said.

'I'm impressed,' I said. 'We've found a wonderful gem in you. A well-cut diamond with just a few rough edges to be polished off. I might get a price from Simpson. Only joking.'

'My pleasure,' Anji said. 'I can't think of a better job and the best mentors.'

'Nice speech,' I said. 'Especially when you have other things on your mind.'

Anji blushed.

'Don't tease the girl,' Cherry admonished. 'Now give this Beamer some welly!'

* * *

When we arrived back, Arthur was waiting for us with Albert Archer of Abacus Detective Agency of 'you can count on us' fame. The two men had had some time to get to know each other while we were journeying back from Zeus. They had decided that Archer would call Arthur by his wrestling name of 'Dangerous', there being too many As knocking around.

Archer reminded me of a weasel, his Roman nose looked to have the contours of a snout. He was thin as if he needed a good meal or two — time and money being the likely culprits. His clothes needed an update or maybe even a complete revision. This was also, in part, due to the five o'clock shadow at three in the afternoon. The overall look could be described in one word — shabby. Still, he had done a professional job on the Ackroyd case, and he was the sort of guy you would pass in the street and not notice — came in under the radar.

'Nice gaff,' he said.

'We like it,' I said. 'How's business?'

He made that wavy gesture with his right hand. 'You know? So, so. About to pick up, I reckon, or why else would I be here?'

'Normally we would use Arthur for undercover work, but he's a bit noticeable for footwork, and we have other work for him. I was impressed with the dossiers you produced for the Ackroyd business. I'd like to engage your services on four people — three women and one man. We're currently working on getting you the necessary information — names, addresses, telephone numbers, car regs and so on — for you to start. Do the man first, then the women in whatever order that works best for you on the logistics. We'll arrange entry for you to the compound where they work — you and the car will be searched thoroughly, so don't take anything incriminating.'

'Who is your client?' Archer said.

'Zeus.'

'Wow!' he said. 'I suppose you realize this is going to cost you.'

'The last time we did business it was readies over the counter. What's the deal this time?'

'Four hundred a day,' he said tentatively, trying his luck. 'Plus expenses.'

'VAT?'

He made that gesture with his hand again. I interpreted it as a cash deal, like last time. I didn't like it, but it was his funeral if HMRC came calling.

'Agreed. I'd like updates each day. Even sooner, if you uncover something juicy.'

'And what will Dangerous be doing? Can I have any of his time?'

'Dangerous will be watching over us,' I said. 'You're on your own this one.'

'Can I subcontract?'

'Only if they're reliable and discreet.' I said.

'I'll think about it,' he said.

'Think about subcontracting or the whole deal?' I asked.

'The whole deal. Sounds like it might get nasty, especially with you involved. You have a knack of turning up dead bodies.'

I sighed. 'You win. I'll up your fee to five hundred a day.'

He paused for just a second. 'You're on,' he said. 'Let the good times roll.'

CHAPTER SEVEN

'How do I look?' said Cherry, twirling around for me.

She was wearing a long black dress with a halter neck, peep-toe gold sandals with high heels, and a gold chain around her neck: from the chain hung a gold heart — that had been a present from me. I felt pleased with my choice. Everything kept simple, because she needed nothing. Her make-up was light, showing the coffee-cream of her skin. Her hair was scraped back and held by two tortoiseshell grips.

'Ravishing,' I said. 'You're going to knock them dead.'

'Don't use that expression, Nick. It might be tempting fate. You look good, too,' she said. 'Black dinner jacket, matching trousers, white shirt with frills down the front, black patent leather shoes and a maroon bow tie. As they say, you scrub up well.'

There was a knock on the door. Our transport had arrived.

It wasn't just transport, it was a shiny black Rolls Royce with a driver complete with cap. He saluted us and opened the door for Cherry. Same for me on the other side. We glided smoothly away and lounged back in the deep seats. There was a smell of leather, like it was brand new and the protective covers had just been taken off. Luxury.

The Roller pulled up at the top of the hill outside a Palladian mansion with a commanding view of the greenery of Hampstead Heath. If you had to live in London, then this was the place to be. Forget Mayfair and Park Lane and their city enclaves: sit here in the garden and sip an iced drink while letting a sunset panorama wash over you.

The chauffeur got out of his seat and opened the rear doors. Cherry and I climbed out to be met by a man of about sixty in a black three-piece suit. He led us up from the exterior steps into a wide hall. It had an airy feel about it that was comforting; no chance of claustrophobia here and a promise of many rooms to explore. A long staircase wound its way to the second floor of three, judging by the windows that could be seen from outside. There were several doors leading off the hall, and he led us to one at the back of the house. Inside was a capacious drawing room. The room was decorated in subtle pink with several sofas in a print of peacocks against a background of sugar cane.

And there, standing up and looking out of the French doors leading to the garden, were Sir Gerald and Lady Livia Campion. She was dressed in a pale-yellow trouser suit in silk with flared legs. She could have just stepped out of a back issue of *Vogue*. She looked, at first glance, to be in her early fifties, but on closer inspection reality kicked in. Her forehead was fixed in a permanent expression of surprise, her unlined eyes showed a face that was impossibly taut, her lips too plump. Her hair, no hint of grey, was cut in a classic bob that had echoes of Audrey Hepburn.

And there, completely the opposite of his role as one of power in the corporate world, stood Campion. In shoes, too. Concession for Lady Livia? This was role reversal to the limit. It was clear from his demeanour that this was a relationship where Livia called the shots.

'Snetterton,' said Livia to the man in black, 'some drinks for our guests. Champagne, I think. Yes, champagne cocktails. We'll have them in the garden.'

Snetterton nodded his head and glided silently out of the room as if on roller skates or doing an impersonation of Parker from *Thunderbirds*.

'Stop drooling, Gerald,' she said, seeing her husband staring at Cherry. 'It doesn't become you.' Turning to me, she said, 'So you must be Shannon. Pray introduce us to your companion.'

I could sense an air of jealousy in her tone. Campion simply stared at Cherry, his eyes fixed on her in wonder. *How can one woman be so beautiful?* he would be thinking.

'This is Cherry,' I said. 'Life companion and business partner.'

'Delighted to meet you,' she said. 'Have you come far?'

'We have a place in Docklands,' I said.

'How very dreary for you,' she said. 'Full of oiks, is it?'

'Can't walk up the street without tripping over at least three,' I said.

'Now you're teasing me, Shannon. I can't tell whether you are joking or not.'

'That's easy,' said Cherry. 'When his lips are moving, he's joking.'

'Now you're doing it,' Livia said.

'I told you he would be fun,' Campion said. 'Furthermore, I get the impression that no one can pull the wool over Shannon's eyes. He's just what we need. Too little fun nowadays, and too many hiding their real feelings.'

'Let's start again,' I said. 'Please call me Nick.'

'Maybe later,' she said. 'Until I get to know you, I will call you Shannon. 'Your companion is . . . ?'

'Walker,' said Cherry. 'And what do we call you?'

'Ma'am and sir.'

Well, this was going to be fun.

Snetterton arrived back and we followed him into the garden and sat at a wooden table on wicker chairs with deep cushions and started sipping our drinks. Whatever you could say about Snetterton — and I probably would when Cherry and I recounted the dinner — he made a mean champagne cocktail. Didn't stint on the brandy.

'Blankets, Snetterton,' Livia said. 'There is a chill to the air.'

'Pretty garden,' I said. 'What a display of roses — which is the extent of my gardening knowledge — such perfume, too.'

I'm good on grass, too, on thinking about it, and this was good grass. Manicured to within an inch of its life, with those stripes you only get with an old-fashioned lawnmower. 'You must have green fingers, ma'am.'

'Oh, no,' Livia said. 'We have a gardener for that.'

'Any other staff apart from Snetterton and the gardener?' I asked.

'Just Cook and a housemaid, and the chauffeur, of course,' Campion said, making his second contribution to the conversation as alcohol went to work on his system. 'They all live in and have rooms in the servants' quarters on the top floor. Had them so long they're like family.'

'I wouldn't go that far,' corrected Livia. 'Ah, here's Snetterton with the blankets. Dependable, is Snetterton.'

We were each given a tartan blanket like the ones you would take on a picnic. Snetterton restrained himself from tucking one around ma'am's knees as too fussy even for him.

'Campion tells me that you are different to others in the industry,' Livia said. 'He says that he can trust you. That, certainly, is refreshing. It only took one minute, he said, and he knew you were special.'

'I'm honoured,' I said, 'for his trust and for the opportunity of meeting you.'

'You've met our daughters,' she said.

'Like in *King Lear*,' said Campion. 'Goneril, Regan and Cordelia.'

But which one was Cordelia?

'What do you make of them?' Livia asked.

'Fine, upstanding women. You should be proud of them. Three individuals all with the same dream.'

'Of course they're not Campion's,' said Livia dismissively. 'They're from another marriage of mine. It will be the end of an era when Campion passes. No male line, the bloodline over. The son he always wanted was doomed never to be.'

'Who will take over the business?' said Cherry, managing to get a word in edgeways. 'Any preferences?'

'Shapiro more or less runs the show now, underneath me acting as chairman,' said Campion. 'He will stay. The three girls will each sit under him, each managing a division. Probably simply moving up and/or sideways from their current positions. Unless you recommend that one or more of them is unfit.'

'That's a heavy load to put on Shannon's shoulders,' Cherry said.

'His history suggests that he is used to that,' said Campion. 'I want everything shipshape before I go.' God, this was getting morbid, I thought. 'Once you've finished the Gambling Division, you can move on to the next two. That should keep you busy for a while. Ah, I hear the bell. Dinner is served.'

Campion led us back into the drawing room and then through the door opposite into the dining room. The room had oak panelling to waist height and above that some subtle shade of cream. There was a long table that seated twelve with our four places laid at one end with a view over the garden. There was a chandelier centred over the table — who, without taste, wouldn't want a chandelier in a mansion like this? Someone — the maid, I guessed — had lit the fire to take away the evening chill. The clock on the mantlepiece said eight o'clock precisely. All very proper.

'Wine, Snetterton,' Campion said. 'I've chosen a crisp Chablis to go with the fish — Livia's favourite salmon — and a Pomerol to accompany my favourite — roast beef. The Pomerol has been decanted and breathing since this morning and will be nicely mellow by now.'

Snetterton filled our glasses with the white wine and went to stand at the wall closest to the door in case there were any further demands. Nice intimate chat? I don't think so.

The Chablis was as crisp as promised and was served with gravadlax and sliced avocado with a mustard and dill sauce. Not much culinary skill from Cook there. More like flower arranging.

'Did you ever doubt, sir,' I said, 'that you would finish up ruling an empire?'

'My father was the second generation,' Campion said. 'A hard taskmaster — I suppose I take after him in that respect — the sins of the father and all that. He made me start at the bottom of the business — mostly print media in those days and a few betting shops — and work my way up when I had proved myself at that level. The third generation — my generation — is supposed to be the one where everything falls apart — from rags to riches and then back again in three generations, they say. I always hoped to prove them wrong.'

Snetterton, seamlessly refilled our glasses and went back to his position by the door. Campion continued.

'Father was made a lord for his contribution to the freedom of the press — and, I suspect, for his contribution to the party's funds.'

'Campion is hoping to become a lord, too,' Livia said. 'That would cap his career, and he could then retire gracefully. The one last tick on the list of desires that has driven him for so long.'

Snetterton left the room briefly to call for the maid to clear the dishes and prepare to bring in the beef. She brought in dishes of vegetables — peas, broccoli and roast potatoes — a deep bowl of horseradish sauce and a jug of gravy — and was followed by Cook wheeling in a domed trolley just like they did at a gentlemen's club. She slid back the lid to reveal six Yorkshire puddings and a joint of rib of beef. Snetterton carved — no one asked how we would like it — and placed two thick slices to myself, Cherry and Campion and one thin slice for Livia. She forewent the Yorkshire pudding, too, and was still only taking small sips of the Chablis. When the laden plates had been placed on the table before us, Snetterton poured a small amount of the Pomerol in Campion's glass for him to test. 'Nectar,' he pronounced. Snetterton then filled our large crystal goblets and went back to his station by the door. For a moment there was silence. I waited for the inevitable. Livia broke first.

'And so,' she said, 'was prison as bad as they say? I've never known a criminal before. I only know what I've seen on the television. *Porridge* and the like.'

'If you were thinking jolly japes, then that is nothing like the truth. It is hard. Cells full of pent-up testosterone. At any moment there is a risk of an explosion and an attack on whoever was in the way at the time. You could cut the electric atmosphere with a butterknife.' I took a sip of the Pomerol — as smooth as Campion had promised. 'Forget about prison being a way of reform. It is simply a hotbed of training for future crime. It's the foundation of recidivism. No one leaves prison unscathed.'

Cherry came to my rescue.

'As we're on to personal subjects,' Cherry said to Livia, 'what is your goal in life, ma'am? What is the one thing you have to do before the Grim Reaper calls?'

'I was brought up not to dream, but to be single-minded. Set your goals, and then pursue them with unwavering determination.'

'The power behind the throne?' Cherry asked. She had Livia in her sights now. Cherry was the one with determination.

'Despite the myth espoused by men, we live in a matri-archal society. It is women who call the shots. Isn't that true, Campion?'

'If you say so, darling,' he said, proving her point.

The plates were cleared and the meal was finished with a sherry trifle with the accent on the word sherry. This was breathalyser strength.

'It is time for us to withdraw, Walker,' Livia said, 'and leave the men to their tedious talk of business. I want to know all about you. And about Shannon, too.'

'Coffee in the drawing room, madam?' said Snetterton.

'Excellent, Snetterton,' she replied, 'and some petit fours.'

To go with the petit bourgeoisie, I thought. Cherry had drawn the short straw. The Spanish Inquisition would seem lenient when compared to Livia's questioning, I was sure.

When they had left the room and Snetterton had returned from ordering the coffees, he said to Campion, 'Brandies, sir?'

'Bring the decanter,' Campion said, 'and leave it on the table. Two of the large glasses, too. Tell Cook she has put on a good show.'

Snetterton nodded and appeared moments later with the brandy decanter — why did you need a decanter for brandy? It doesn't need to breathe or have any extraneous stuff at the bottom — complete with one of those silver labels around its neck for those who are forgetful or who have no sense of smell. Campion poured a liberal measure into our brandy balloons.

Snetterton brought in a humidor and Campion chose one of the fat cigars. Snetterton clipped the end with a tool from the box. Campion had it lit and took a deep breath. He smiled and exhaled a thick plume of smoke.

He leaned back in the chair, slipped his shoes off, took a sip of the brandy and sighed. 'The world is passing me by,' he said. 'I'm a tyrannosaurus rex living in an age of circuitry, unable to fully understand the mechanics of social media and electronic publishing. If I get the terminology right, I am an analogue man in a digital world. My sole purpose — and a very important purpose — is to charm the City and, from that, to reward the shareholders.'

Gosh, this was getting heavy. But I knew why I was being privileged with these confidences. It sent a chill up my spine.

'So, you're seeing the writing on the wall?' I said. 'Time to bow out gracefully?'

'I think so. Pass the burden on to someone else. Shapiro could handle it, but it would be outside his comfort zone.'

'Recruit someone external who can cope with the demands? What does Livia think about it?'

'You don't really need to ask that question, do you?' he said, quaffing more brandy.'

'Internal promotion,' I said. 'But which one to take the reins? Which one of the three daughters?'

'The three witches of Macbeth. Natural selection à la Darwin will out,' he said. 'I suspect Livia has her favourite, but whoever takes control will be fine with her. The empire passed down to one of her daughters. The end of an era. The start of a new one.'

We were interrupted by Snetterton announcing that the chauffeur was waiting to drive us home. Cherry and Livia were already in the hall, Livia having decided the timing, I had no doubt. We said our goodnights and thanks for a memorable evening. *Memorable* being the best euphemism we could come up with after so much alcohol. We were silent during the journey, knowing that the chauffeur could be listening to every word and reporting back to Livia.

Once home, we went straight to our floor at the very top of the building and started to get ready for bed. My head was woozy. Cherry was taking her time as if her mind was elsewhere.

'Did you get a grilling from Livia?' I enquired. 'That was a long time to be ensconced on your own with her.'

'It wasn't about me,' Cherry replied. 'It was all about you. Question after question, like she was compiling a dossier about you. She sees you as a threat against her master plan for her daughters. You know what is behind all this, don't you?'

'The strength of my new relationship with Campion,' I said. 'I suspect he may want to use me as a buffer between them and Shapiro. Keep them in check. Full-time role in the company.'

'It's more than that, isn't it?' she said. 'Shall I say it or you?'

'Let me,' I said. 'It's me that's the problem.'

'And the problem is?'

'I'm the son he never had.'

'Precisely.'

CHAPTER EIGHT

Valentine had been busy and had security passes ready for Dangerous and Archer: why Zeus had passes that didn't need photo ID, I didn't know. Just part of an overall laxness in the systems in the company, especially given the supposed risk of saboteurs. Penny pinching? I made a mental note to include security issues in our final report.

He had also collected the data we had requested from Rose and had his laptop and the company computer warming up. The final result of his endeavours was to set up an interview with an 'expert' and the watcher of the betting team. The more I saw of Valentine, so self-effacing, modest and untouched by his beauty, and the work he had produced, the more I liked him and had empathy for him, in what must have been an awkward position where everyone thought he had got the job through nepotism. On top of that he had a creative mind and a gift for lateral thinking which was essential for our line of work.

'I was impressed by your thoughts about the casinos,' I said. 'I'd like you and Anji to repeat the exercise for the betting shops. See if there is a pattern in common. From there, we'll start to see if there are any links between the odds quoted and the losses incurred by them. First, coffee.'

'I'll go,' said Valentine.

'I'll go with him,' said Anji, unsurprisingly. 'I can help carry them back.'

As they left the room, my phone gave two pings meaning there were two new messages. Both Albert and Dangerous reporting that they were in position. I hoped that Albert had had better luck than me in finding a car park space near to where Selby's car would be in its allotted parking space, so he could follow as soon as the car left — I was at a far corner, a trot from the front entrance and, stupidly, I liked to be able to see the Beamer and make sure she was OK. Seemed silly, but cars are always female in my book and needed to be treated as such, with love and respect.

'What are you hoping to get from the interview of the so-called expert and the watcher bod?' Cherry asked.

'I'm not sure; it's not much more than a fact-finding mission. The performance of the betting side is a puzzle,' I said. 'The odds should always be in the bookies' favour. Yes, you can have a bad run, but in the long term the bookie always wins. A year of bad results is long term. Freak events should have evened out. There is an imbalance somewhere, something is niggling in my brain. An itch I can't scratch.'

'Maybe I can help you.'

'I'll play good cop this time,' I said. 'It might confuse them if they've been briefed by Rose or Petunia.'

'Whatever you say, Shannon.'

'We'll do this on our own. Don't want to seem mob-handed, and Valentine and Anji have plenty to do.'

Valentine had got us a small conference room and Terry Baxter — expert — and Sally Green — watcher — were already there waiting for us. 'So good of you to see us,' I said, 'you must have many more important things to do.'

'At your service,' said Green.

She was dressed in an unflattering trouser suit that had wide legs finishing four inches above her flat-heeled, lace-up black shoes. Her hair was greasy, as if she hadn't washed it for a while, and was cut in boyish style. She needed a designer guru to take her in hand. She was wearing a large pair of glasses with tortoiseshell rims that gave her the appearance of an owl. Geeksville, USA. I put her age at about mid-thirties, so she should have had enough experience to know what she was talking about.

I put Baxter's age at around forty — so, experienced, too. He had an unruly beard that would have benefitted from a good trim. Being a back-room bod, there was no dress code, and so he was wearing a pair of classic 501 denim jeans to go with a T-shirt with the name of an obscure heavy metal band that I had never heard of and was never likely to — with luck.

'Can I send someone out for coffee?' I said.

'I'm fine,' said Walker — we were in work mode now, surnames only. 'Let's get on with it.'

'Yes. Get on with it. Yes,' I said. 'Do excuse my colleague. She was at the back of the queue when God handed out patience.' I gave a smile for what was a very small bit of humour. 'As context, how many teams like yours are there?'

'There's us on horse racing — that's the most popular — then working downwards, football, rugby, cricket, tennis, greyhounds and specials — that's unusual bets.'

'I'm curious,' I said, 'but how does one get into a job like yours?'

'I come from a horsey family,' said Sally Green. 'Daddy was a trainer. Racing was in my blood. After university, I got a cub reporter's job on the sports section of the *Mirror*. Got more involved and better at it until I made it up to racing journalist. While there, I read every racing fact, devoured the form book, ran through the statistics and saw an opportunity to use my skills here. I built up my contacts — scouts, we call them . . .'

'I'd call them snouts,' Cherry said.

'Whatever,' said Green. 'More pay here, so I took it. End of story.'

'Similar to Sally,' Baxter said, 'except I didn't have any family to help me get on the ladder. I got a statistics degree and set out to be an actuary . . .'

Cherry interrupted again. 'Don't they say an actuary is someone who finds accountancy too exciting?'

Baxter sighed. 'It's an old joke,' he said, 'but has some truth. From there I worked behind the scenes on the televising of horse racing. Built up my knowledge and was asked to do a bit of pundit work. I soon realized that I was not one for being on the screen or radio. Saw this job advertised. Good pay. Do what I love doing. Not many people have those kinds of opportunities.'

Walker blatantly looked at her watch.

'So how does the system work for you two?' I asked. 'Where does it start?'

'Good question,' Green said. 'We're a team. We overlap a lot. How much do you know?'

'I'm a complete novice,' I said. 'Back to basics, please.'

'Let's just go through the journey,' Green said. 'So, you have a race. OK? The computer makes its assessment on odds based on the past times a horse has run. It factors in the jockey, the going of the ground — heavy, good — combined weight of jockey and handicap weight, length of race, whether the course is clockwise or anticlockwise and a whole host of other variables. Then we step in. Either from our gut feel or information from the scouts, we pass those odds or we change them. You know the sort of thing. I'm first in line. I make my assessment of the computer's crunching and decide whether that seems to be passable, or make a decision on what the odds should now be.'

'Then that decision comes to me,' said Baxter. 'Do I feel that there is sufficient evidence to overrule the computer? We two sit down together and talk about it. Most of the calculations only require a glance. For the rest we come to a joint decision. Adjust the odds, if necessary. It's a great life.'

'So,' Walker said, 'what would it take to adjust the odds falsely upwards and tell some bad people to bet on that horse?'

'It could be done,' Baxter said, 'but risky. You'd have to get both of us to cooperate. What would happen if Sally said to me that we could make some quick money? If I said no, I could report it and that would be the end of the job for her. End of career, too. Who would want to employ a person with a cloud of fraud, of dishonesty, hanging over their heads?'

'I suppose,' I said, 'that if Sally, say, seemed short of cash — economizing on things, smaller car, downsizing house, bringing in her own lunch, drinking the awful coffee here instead of going out and so on — it might present an opportunity for fraudulent acts. These sorts of things often start out as a bit of a joke, a bit of fun. Then the idea takes wings and the act is done. If it works the first time, then it becomes regular. You're caught in the system.'

'You would have to know someone with sufficient cash to profit from it,' said Green.

'Or people, plural,' said Walker.

'Maybe a syndicate, say,' I said. 'The more you get people to invest, the more your cut. The more your involvement, the more you are worth.'

'Sounds good to me,' Walker said.

'Tell me,' I said, 'why were you picked for this interview?'

'Get real, Shannon,' said Walker. 'This is some kind of whitewash. Get the two most honest employees to present themselves. Isn't that right, Baxter? Isn't that right, Green? Makes me feel like something is going on.'

'I'm sure that's not the case,' I said. 'You are reading too much into this.'

'Thank you,' said Green.'

'Where,' I said, 'does Petunia fit into the picture?'

'Makes the odd decision to intervene. Does it as a watching brief. A kind of final quality control, I suppose one would say.'

'And what about Selby?' I said.

There was a telling silence.

'He sits above Petunia. Oversees everything. Keeps tab on her. Checks up on us to make sure everything is right. That it's legitimate.'

'Does he ever change your decisions or make his own suggestion?'

'Rarely,' said Green.

'Which means sometimes,' said Walker.

Again, there was silence.

'One last thing,' I said. 'I need a surefire horse, each way bet at middle odds — say six to one or above. Any tips?'

'There's a meeting at Plumpton on Monday,' Green said. 'Small track, less influence on the odds. Golden Boy in the three-thirty. You should get your money back and a bit of profit.'

'Thank you both,' I said.

Walker grunted.

We left the room, wiser but less popular.

* * *

We went back to our room to join Anji and Valentine. 'Debrief,' I said. 'Will you do the honours, Walker?'

'We have a situation where fraud is possible — not proven, but possible,' she said. 'Two people — expert and watcher — could collude to give longer odds than calculated by the computer algorithm. They could justify it by claiming inside knowledge. From there, somebody — probably a syndicate as you would need serious money to make it worthwhile — could back the horse and make a profit. There would be no guarantee that that horse would win on that occasion, but in the long term the syndicate would show a profit by the odds being in its favour. It's playing the bookie at its own game.'

'Statistically, you're on to a winner,' I said. 'Our job will be to search for examples of where this may have happened and find the team, or teams, I suppose, involved. Establish where there are incidents where a particular team is running losses or small profits on balance. It's going to be a slog, but we'll start with the last month and work back in time until we're sure of the facts. Gains or losses on a ten-pound bet. We're basically making comparisons between the teams to see who performs worse. Like I say it will be a slog — needles and haystacks — but this is how we justify our fee.'

'Before we start,' said Cherry, 'have you been able to get anywhere with the betting shops?'

'Another slog,' said Anji. 'From what we've found so far — and there's more checking to do — it seems like the same pattern as the casinos: profits skewed towards those close to London. But, as I said, more work to do before we can be sure.'

'Plan of action,' I said. 'Anji and Valentine, finish your analysis of the betting shops. Cherry and I will start on the team analysis, although she will have to break off as she has lunch planned with the witches. Anyone have a preference of sport?'

'I'm into football,' said Valentine. 'Maybe I could do that.'

'Tennis,' said Anji. 'I used to play a bit as a kid. Still follow the big tournaments.'

'OK,' I said. 'Cherry?'

'Cricket,' she said. 'That's where I will be the least unknowledgeable, if that makes sense.'

'Then I'll take horse racing,' I said. 'Valentine, we're going to need more computers, so we can each access the computer mainframe.'

'I'm on it,' he said, getting up and leaving the room.

'I'll get the coffee,' Anji said. 'We're going to need lots.'

'Then let's go for it,' I said, clapping my hands. 'Go, go, go.'

* * *

Campion phoned me and asked me to meet him for a sandwich lunch to talk over progress to date. It would have been rude to turn down the offer, even though it left Anji and Valentine on their own in the swamp that was crunching figures. I told them to take a walk at lunchtime to give their eyes and brains a rest.

Campion's office was obscenely large — you could have held a cricket match in there, and that's only a slight exaggeration. There was a conference table for twelve with some spare chairs when needed. An informal sitting area of four sofas in olive green leather set around two glass-topped coffee tables. His desk continued the office theme of smoked glass and chrome that I had already seen during my interviews. On the top was an antique desk tidy out of which I could see the white snow-cap of a Mont Blanc fountain pen and a glass bottle of blue ink. As Valentine would say, 'Cool'.

Campion stood up from one of the sofas and shook my hand: he did that thing of placing his left hand on top of my right as we were doing so. He gestured me to sit opposite him with a platter of sandwiches, plates, napkins, a bottle of red wine and two crystal glasses between us. He poured the wine, took a sip, leaned back in his sofa and looked across at me.

'Good to see you again,' he said.

'And you, too, sir,' I replied.

'I think we can drop the "sir" when it's just the two of us,' he said. 'Made any progress so far, my boy?'

'It's early days, yet. We've got a few leads, though. Mostly, we're deep in analysing numbers looking for patterns. It's that rudimentary phase which is all about detail. That will be the foundation stone upon which we will build our conclusions.'

He started to help himself to some of the array of sandwiches that would have fed four, but Campion had a healthy appetite, from what I had seen at the dinner. There were some beef and horseradish sandwiches which I left for him, as I knew they would be his favourite. I settled for a prawn mayo and a BLT.

'How's that lad of Shapiro's doing?' Campion asked. 'He seems a quiet sort of boy. I don't get much impression of him.'

'He's doing fine. He needs a mentor badly if he is to make any progress. Whether you find one or not, you will get back more than you gave to us. He's got a good brain, more than you would think from a second-class degree in Sociology. Doesn't really equip you for much. He needs stretching, but nobody teaches him anything. He can't lose the brand of being Shapiro's son. No one trusts him — he's seen as a spy in the camp. He'd be best to move on. He's done something since graduation now: you could write him a good reference. That could put him up the list above other candidates. Frankly, he's wasted here. How will Shapiro react when I have to answer his question about the boy?'

'How do fathers feel about their sons? He'll take it badly. He wants Valentine to follow him in his shoes, only better. Build a ladder to the stars and climb on everyone. Isn't that how the song goes?'

'Tricky,' I said.

'And what about my stepdaughters? You've had time to think since our dinner. What do you make of them?'

'Ambitious.' I said, hoping that would be the end of the conversation.

'Ambitious in a good way or a bad way?'

'Depends on your point of view,' I said.

'You're avoiding my question, Nick,' he said, 'and it's one that you will have to answer sooner or later.'

'I'd prefer later,' I said.

'Your silence speaks volumes,' he said.

'I'll know in a while,' I said. 'Walker is taking them to lunch. I'd like to park my judgement till I know more.'

'You're stalling. You don't want to upset me, but I'll give you more time. Stalling isn't the same as hesitation. People stall for a reason, and they hesitate when they have no answer. I value your opinion. Don't drag it out. Now, on matters of more urgency. Do you want that last roast beef sandwich?'

* * *

Walker looked one step away from a meltdown when she arrived back from her fact-finding mission. 'The things I do for you, Shannon.'

'My incredible powers of perception tell me it didn't go well,' I said.

'What a trio,' she said. 'It was like that Cerberus from Greek mythology. The many-headed dog protecting the underworld. We should change their name from the three witches to the three bitches. It was like the Spanish Inquisition without the language problem. Three at a time. Question after question. They learned more from me than I did from them.'

'It was worth a shot,' I said. 'Did you build any bridges?'

'Any bridges I got were burned to the ground immediately after. They are impossible to deal with. They speak as one. They act as one. I had such trouble knowing who was who, despite their different fashion styles. I invented a way to tell them apart. From now on, Violet will be Casinov — like Russian — "casino" with "V" for Violet: Rose will be Robs — Rose with the betting shops. Petunia will be Petuniao, like in Portuguese, pronounced *ow* at the end as if hitting your finger with a hammer. For their description, we have Casinov with her blue eyes, Robs with her mutton and Petunia with her drab clothes.'

'Do you think their fashion sense is different so they appear separate, rather than a combined force that threatens outsiders?' I said.

'They want only one thing,' Walker said, 'and that is to completely run the whole business, and they won't take prisoners on the way to the top.'

'Any weaknesses that we can target?' I said.

'They've only one thing that worries them. You. I sensed fear along with their dislike of you. Something is going down. Something you might discover.'

'Then we are on the right track. There is something to search for. All we have to do is find it.'

'You make it sound easy,' said Walker.

'All we have to do is keep digging. Someone, somewhere, will have made a mistake. Show us the door and leave it open for us. Did you get any idea of what's bugging them about me?'

'Apart from the normal, you mean? Arrogance, obstinacy, permanently joking and all that stuff, you mean? It's your ability to follow a new course that no one has considered till now. They can't read you, so they can't predict what you will do, and that is what they fear.'

'And how was the meal? Any plus points about the food to save the day?'

'They took me to a Greek restaurant which, under other circumstances, would be passable. The kleftiko hadn't been cooked long enough, so it wasn't falling off the bone. The houmous was too salty, designed to increase the volume of alcohol you drank, the pastries were soggy. All in all, it only survived because it was the only place within walking distance of the Zeus complex.'

'So,' I said, 'to sum up, it one of the worst lunches you have ever been to.'

'Again, what perception you have. Hit the nail on the head.'

'I'll make it up to you when this business is over.'

'How about tonight? Takeaway Chinese, two bottles of Chardonnay and an early night?'

'Sounds perfection. Let's do it.'

'I'll take that as a promise,' she said with a gleam in her eye. 'No backing out now.'

'I don't have my fingers crossed. You're on.'

* * *

We came down in the lift with Selby. He didn't look pleased to see us. Fair enough: we were the enemy, as our presence might bring about a culling among staff, maybe him, too. If we couldn't find a way around the decline in profits, then the only thing to do was to cut overheads, which, as the biggest proportion, meant wages, which meant people. Selling the Betting Division might be an option, but would the new owner want the services of a failed manager? Rhetorical question.

The presence of Anji and Cherry should have brought a smile to Selby's face. If you were in a low mood, the sight of my two sidekicks should have mellowed him. Such beauty.

The world should have been a better place for seeing them. The sun will always bring a smile in the face of perfection.

Thankfully, we reached the ground floor without Selby venting his spleen. As we came to exit the building, Anji stopped. 'Hell,' she said, 'I've left my phone in the office. Won't be a sec.' She scurried away, leaving Cherry and I with nothing to do. I went out of the building and looked around the car park. I saw Arthur's white van keeping watch on us. In the row a way back from Selby's car, was a shabby Ford Fiesta that could only be Archer's. All present and correct.

Selby passed me and came to his people carrier — practical choice of a family car, I assumed, for the wife and three children — in the allotted space. I saw the lights blink when he pressed his remote key. He got in and I walked towards his car. He pressed the ignition.

Then there was a loud explosion and I was blown off my feet. Selby's car burst into flames.

And that was the end of Selby.

CHAPTER NINE

They had to send two fire engines as the blaze from Selby's car spread to those surrounding it, petrol tanks exploding, flames everywhere. It touched the visitor's space where I should have been. Boy, had we been lucky!

I had been lifted into the air and landed on the ground. I shook my head to clear it, picked myself up and looked around for Cherry. She was lying on the floor a couple of paces in front of me. She would have experienced more of the blast than I had. She wasn't moving. I got down to the ground, cradled her head and checked her vital signs. She was breathing and had a pulse. I could hear the wail of ambulance and police sirens. Thank God! I prayed she would be all right.

An ambulance medic came over to us, examined Cherry and called for a stretcher. He and his female colleague lifted her on to the stretcher and wheeled her over to the ambulance. A policeman assessed the scene. I made to get into the ambulance with Cherry when the policeman stopped me.

'Sorry, sir,' he said, 'but this is now a major incident scene. No one comes in and no one goes out. Back into the building, please.'

'She'll be alright,' said one of the ambulance crew. 'Don't worry.'

What a stupid thing to say — don't worry. How in God's name could I not worry? I walked back in the building and found Valentine and Anji sitting on a sofa in the reception area. 'How are you both?' I said. 'Unhurt? Please say yes.'

They both nodded. 'We were way back from the blast,' said Anji. Then it struck her. 'Where's Cherry?'

'Off to hospital,' I said. 'She wasn't conscious. The police wouldn't let me go with her. Apparently, this is now a major incident. Probably sabotage, I would have thought, judging by the history here.'

But there was doubt in my mind. I could think about that later. Now there were more pressing matters. 'Whatever the police are going to do, I need it done fast, so I can get to Cherry as soon as possible.'

I looked around and saw Archer approaching. He had a mixed expression on his face, part relief but mostly frightened.

'We need to talk,' he said.

'Agreed,' I said, 'but not now. You need to do some swift thinking of a good reason why you are here, otherwise the police will regard you as a suspect and we'll be in a lot of trouble and sitting in separate cells so we don't have the same story.'

'I didn't sign up for this kind of situation,' he said.

'Not now, Archer,' I said. 'Not now. Cherry is in hospital and that's my only concern. I'll ring you with a time we can all meet up. Now, mingle with the crowd so you're not linked to us. Move it.'

As Archer peeled away, I saw Arthur — Dangerous, how ironic. No one could miss him. He stood out from the crowd by height alone. The police would see his bulk and he would be among the first to be interviewed.

'I saw them wheel Cherry away, Nick,' he said. 'What's going on?'

The doubt in my mind was replaced by certainty.

'We've got ourselves mixed up in something much bigger than we thought. As usual, we may have been the catalyst for the bad guys to act. As far as Cherry goes, I'm in the same boat as all of you. No word of her. Be a while for that, I think. Fingers crossed, everyone.'

'What am I supposed to say as the reason why I'm here?' Arthur said.

'There are options: fabricate a convincing story or come clean. If we start lying, I think we will be found out and it would be suspicious. I think we're going to have to tell the truth. You were here watching our backs. Let's call it standard behaviour at the beginning of a job. Turns out we've been proven right.'

'I think I saw it all,' he said.

'Tell me what you saw, or what you think you saw?'

'Part way through the morning,' Arthur said, 'a white van, bigger than mine, Bedford, I think, pulled in front of Selby's car, obscuring the view. The van had a sign on the sides: TJ Mobile Tyre Services. That was how they had a reason for being there. I didn't think anything of it at the time, but it all makes sense now.'

'We have to report this, Arthur,' I said. 'Get one of the police over here. There's lots of them milling around taking contact data.'

Anji had tears in her eyes. She came across to me and put an arm around my shoulder. Squeezed me tightly. The comfort was flowing between us. Her to me, me to her. 'Can I come with you when you go to the hospital?' she said.

'Thanks for the sentiment and the support, Anji, but there may be things I need to say to her in private. Valentine, look after this girl. Keep her safe while all of this is working out.'

When you want a police officer they're like buses: either none around or they come in packs of a dozen. As Arthur queued up to speak to one of the policemen, I turned to face the door to the building. That's when I saw him.

DI Dennis Palmer!

We had crossed swords on the law firm case when he regarded me as the prime suspect for murder. At the end of the case, we had sorted out our differences and worked together as a team to catch the culprits. I wondered what he would make of my presence here, the site of another murder.

As he wended his way across the reception area, I saw how little he had changed in the few months since we had last met. He was fifty-five years old, coming up to retirement, and all he wanted was a quiet life. He was six feet tall and barrel-chested, dressed in a neatly pressed grey suit and a gleaming white shirt: the plain blue tie had a perfect Windsor knot. His grey hair was receding at the temples and his eyes were brown. More to the point, he had a serious OCD problem — everything neat and tidy and in its place, even though in the law case, he had disturbed the crime scene by lining up the pencils on the murdered man's desktop.

'Shannon,' he said. 'I thought that I had seen the last of you — what did I ever do wrong to deserve this? — and here you are again at the scene of a murder. What is it with you? Corpses seem to follow you around.'

'I'll tell you all in a moment once we've done a deal,' I said. 'Hopefully, you can cut me some slack. I'll tell you all for one favour.'

'Which is?' he said doubtfully.

'Cherry was caught up in the blast. She's in hospital and I need to be by her side. The deal is that we both go to see her and, at that time, I will tell you the whole story. There's big things going down here that you need to be aware of, that are pertinent to wrapping everything up. If it's no deal, I clam up while the murderer gets away. What do you say?'

'I could charge you with withholding evidence,' he said. 'Give you a couple of nights in the cells. No hospital then.'

'But you're not going to do that, are you?' I said. 'Why pass up what could be vital information to get you hot on the heels of the murderers? We're wasting time, Palmer. What do you say? I'll tell you what. Let me give you something on account.' I caught Arthur's eye and beckoned him over to join us. 'OK, Arthur. Tell the nice policeman what you saw.'

'I'm honoured to meet you, Dangerous,' Palmer said. 'Tell me exactly what you saw?'

Arthur recounted the story and Palmer got out his phone and put out an all-cars bulletin for the van. We didn't have the registration number — who would have any reason to make a note of it? — but the writing on the van's sides should be able to make the search easy.

'I don't know why,' Palmer said, 'but I'll trust you, Shannon. I hope I don't regret it. This better be good. Let's go. My car. I'll put on the lights and sirens. Let's get this show on the road.'

* * *

Palmer's car was an ancient white Ford Sierra, but the outside was spotless, gleaming and sparkling. Inside, there was no dust and none of the usual detritus of sweet wrappers or coffee cups or half-empty bottles of water that you might find in your average family car. Maybe there wasn't a family — kids grown up and left the nest, probably.

With the sirens blaring and the blue lights flashing, it took us only ten minutes to get to the hospital. I remained silent during this time, aware that Palmer could renege on the deal if he got all that he needed from me.

We started at A&E and, with lots of flashing Palmer's warrant card, established that Cherry had been taken to Bluebell Ward. We followed signage and coloured floor routes and found the ward. We pressed a buzzer on the double doors and gained entry. The ward had that distinctive smell of disinfectant that all hospitals have and was bright and shiny and had the look of where you would like to be if you had to be taken to hospital. The nurse who had opened the door led us to a bed at the end of the ward — a good sign, the nearer you are to the nurses' station, the worse is your condition.

'Can you find DI Palmer somewhere private to sit while I concentrate on Cherry?'

'The day room is empty this time of evening. Follow me, sir.'

Cherry, though propped up to a sitting position, seemed to be asleep. There were bruises on her perfect skin and some cuts and grazes which had been treated with purple coloured lotion. I sat in the chair next to her bed and gently took hold of her hand. Her eyelids flickered.

The nurse came back and stood at the foot of the bed.

'How is she doing?' I said, dreading the possible answer.

'She's not in any danger that we can tell.'

That we can tell. What did that mean?

'We think she is just suffering from concussion, but we want to keep her in for a couple of days while we do some scans and run some tests. I don't think you should worry unduly.'

'Will she be able to talk to me when she wakes up?' I asked, dreading the response that the nurse might make.

'We've sedated her to give her a better and quicker chance of recovery. You won't get much from her if she wakes up. She'll be confused, I would have thought. I don't think she will remember much. With luck, she will recognize you. Don't make anything of it if she doesn't. Can I get you a cup of tea? I'm making one for the policeman, so it's no bother.'

'That would be kind,' I said. 'If you could take it to the day room, I'll drink it with the inspector.'

I stroked Cherry's hand tenderly. She opened her eyes and looked at me.

'Who are you?' she said.

'I'm Nick Shannon,' I said. 'We're a couple.'

'A couple of what?' she said.

I didn't know how to express the answer. 'A couple who love each other.'

'What's love?' she said.

'How can I explain this? Love is a constant state of euphoria that means you want to be with someone all the time. It's . . . I don't know.'

'Don't worry about it,' she said with a smile. 'I was only joking. Great to see you, Nick.'

'Gosh, you had me worried. I'll make you pay for that when you get out. What a rotten trick to play. How are you feeling, darling?'

'I have a thumping headache which the painkillers need to work better on. Good to see you're alright. How is everyone?'

'We're all fine,' I said. 'What can you remember?'

'Something to do with Anji's phone. Walking from the building to the car park. Horrific bang — so loud it hurt my ear drums. Ball of fire. Thrown into the air. Next thing, I'm here. What have I missed?'

'The bang was Selby's car. Someone planted a bomb. He didn't stand a chance.'

'Why would someone do such a thing?'

'I'm working on it,' I said. 'With or without the help of DI Palmer. Fate has thrown us together again.'

'Keep your patience,' Cherry said. 'Don't go out of your way to antagonize him.'

The nurse came back to us. 'That's enough for today. She needs sleep. Come back tomorrow.'

I got up from the chair, bent down to her and kissed her on the forehead. 'Till tomorrow. Is there anything I can get you?'

Bad mistake. She reeled off a whole list of things that I was sure to forget, and some that I didn't even know what she was talking about.

'Bye, my darling. Sleep well.'

I went through the thin blue plastic curtains that had given us some visual privacy — everyone in the surrounding beds could hear every word — and made my way to the day room. Palmer, I guessed, had not been idle. The ragtag collection of furniture, which had probably been donated by past patients, was all lined up symmetrically about a small television. Cushions were plumped up. A large, low coffee table had been cleared and sat there with only some sachets of sugar and our two cups of tea on the top.

'How is she?' Palmer said.

'Better than I had feared. The good news is that she can play the violin — which is a great sign, as she couldn't play it before.'

'That's better, Shannon. Back to your old self — which is fine for you, bad for me. Drink your tea like a good boy and tell me everything.'

'It's a long story, one that is still playing out,' I said. 'We are contracted by Zeus to investigate losses in its Gambling Division — the Division of which Selby was in charge. The theory was that fraud might be the cause. We've yet to work that out, but there are certainly opportunities for fraud.'

I paused to drink some tea as my mouth had suddenly gotten dry. Probably nerves after such a devastating event. Maybe even scorched by the heat caused by the bomb. I didn't know. What I did know was that one of Snetterton's stiff brandies would be welcome.

'What we have found out so far is that money laundering is going on at an enormous daily rate. At the casinos, people are buying chips for cash — ten grand per night is one example — and then cashing the proceeds into deposits to bank accounts. One man alone may be laundering two million a year. We've yet to prove it, but I'm convinced it must be happening.'

'Have you told the Fraud Squad about this?' Palmer asked.

'Not yet. We've still to gather evidence they would need to prosecute. Added to that, there is probably laundering going on at betting shops, too. Place bets in cash, move winnings to online accounts which get transferred from there into bank accounts. Again, we can't prove it yet: we need more time to find the evidence. We've only been on our work for a week or so.'

'Any clues as to who is behind it?'

'Not as yet, but we both know where cash of that magnitude comes from.'

'Drugs,' he said.

'Drugs,' I echoed.

'So where does Selby fit into all this?'

'I have two theories,' I said. 'From what I've seen so far, management at Zeus is well below par. Line managers may not have spotted it. Selby should have been in control — it is his sin that is the worst. So, one theory is incompetence.'

'And the other, as if I need to ask?'

'That Selby was taking bribes for turning a blind eye. Maybe he had second thoughts about the money laundering. That's the only other scenario I can see. Then, maybe, the drugs baron is fearful that Selby would go the police and blow the whole business. Planting a bomb in Selby's car would be easy enough for an organization of that size and wealth to put together. Maybe now Selby is dead, they might try for the same arrangement with whoever is replacing him.'

'Anything else?' he asked, although I suspected he knew the answer.

'You asked me whether I had informed the Fraud Squad. There was another reason for not doing so. How much can we trust the Fraud Squad? Cherry, from her past experience there, would echo that. Drug barons often have the police in their pockets. Would we just be signalling to whoever is the mastermind behind it that we know what has just been going on: shut down this operation and move elsewhere?'

'So where do you think we should go from here? You don't seem to have much faith in the police. Fraud Squad, Drugs Squad, whatever.'

'I can trust you, Palmer. Buy me some slack to gather the evidence and work with me while I do it. Like we did on the law case. We were a pretty good team once we sorted out our differences.'

'Do you realize what you're asking me? Withholding evidence from the team working on a murder case?'

'You could retire in a blaze of glory,' I said.'

'Or in disgrace,' he replied.

'Just give me a couple of days. If I can't produce something after that, we go public. Pass everything over. I'll make a full statement and you can handle it from there.'

'I must be a bigger idiot than what my wife thinks. Two days, three at the absolute limit. No extensions. No not keeping me informed. And please,' he said, 'no more dead bodies.'

* * *

We sat in his car and planned our next move. Palmer rang the senior policeman at the Zeus building and got a progress report. Contact details had been collected and those nearest to the car had been interviewed. The building's CCTV cameras had been taken and would need arduous careful watching, because of the long time frame between the time Arthur saw the big van and the bomb exploding. Mrs Selby had been informed and there was a police support officer with her. Although it might be viewed as insensitive, she seemed a good place to start.

It was a short drive from the hospital to the now-fashionable area of Shoreditch. We planned our approach during the ten-minute journey. Palmer would interview Mrs Selby while I would look at items such as bank statements and Selby's computer. We would take away his laptop for an in-detail examination later.

The house was a three-storey Victorian terrace house that looked solidly built but scruffily maintained with some of the paint peeling off the windows. Mrs Selby opened the door. Her eyes were red and there were black areas on her face where her mascara had run. She was dressed in a designer red cashmere dress that clung to her body in all the right places. On her feet were, designer again, a pair of red Louboutin strappy stilettos that even Cherry would have rejected as being a price over the top for a pair of shoes. Two thousand pounds is a hell of a lot of money. Everything seemed incongruous for such an occasion.

She led us into a narrow hall with a set of stairs leading down to a basement and another set for the rooms on the second and third floors. We followed her down to the basement and surveyed the scene. The basement had been remodelled into a state-of-the-art kitchen and dining area. From first glance, it looked like no expense had been spared in the refit. From second glance it looked no different. The worktops were black marble and the units were of Shaker-style oak painted a shade of grey verging on green. There was even an island with three black and chrome high stools where visitors could watch you cooking. Wonderful! The dining area continued the theme with a black tabletop supported by chrome legs. Six director chairs in black leather were placed around the table.

Mrs Selby sat down on a black leather sofa and beckoned us to sit down on another directly opposite. The female police community officer sat beside her. Palmer said, 'If you want a break, Jane, we'll cover everything for a while.' We heard the stairs creak as she walked up and opened the front door — it was cigarette time.

Palmer showed his warrant card and introduced me as being a forensic expert — neat phrasing: not exactly a lie, I was indeed a forensic expert, but not of the type she would think.

'I hate to bother you at such a time, Mrs Selby, but if we are to catch those who murdered your husband, then we need to be quick. Every minute of delay means more time for them to hide away and cover their tracks. Can you think of anyone who had a grudge against Matthew? An enemy, in any terms?'

'No,' she said. 'He wasn't in the sort of job where anyone could want to see him dead. He was just a gambling person. If they were that angry, they would have gone for Matthew's boss, Shapiro. Maybe even Campion. Who knows?'

'How are you coping?' I said. 'You have family?'

'Three children,' she said. 'Eight, ten and twelve. They are devastated. I've arranged for them to board tonight so I can get my head around what has happened.'

Board. Boarding school. *Mucho pesetas.* A picture was forming.

'I'd like to look at some papers that Matthew may have,' I said. 'Does — did — he have a study or office? Would you mind me looking at anything?'

'Top floor,' she said. 'Old servants' quarters. You can't miss it. Papers everywhere. You're welcome to look at anything you want.'

'Thank you,' I said. 'You OK down here, Dennis?'

'Carry on,' he said. 'Send Jane back down while you're at it.'

I walked up stairs. Jane was treating herself to a second cigarette. 'You should go back down now.'

'Before I do,' she said, spinning out the time before having to crush the cigarette under her heel, 'just who the hell are you?'

'An expert in my field. All will become clear in good time. I'll leave you to shut the door.'

I walked up two flights of stairs. The ceilings were lower here. Servants didn't warrant too much headroom. There were three bedrooms squeezed into what would just be loft space in any modern house. The door to the room at the front of the house was partly open. I could see a desk inside that told me this must be Selby's space. I entered.

The room crammed a lot inside: desk, two filing cabinets, an easy chair set in one corner for just sitting and reading, one of those expensive floor lamps that cost a fortune and are supposed to be good enough for surgeons to do a heart transplant over the chair, Anglepoise over the desk and a pinboard on one wall. The walls were painted a dull shade of grey that gave everything a funereal feel.

The desk was covered in paper that I took to be pending, given there were two three-drawer filing cabinets that I would have thought could handle this volume of paper. Among the groaning pile of paper was a laptop that grinned excitedly at me. If it wasn't password protected, I could power up and access everything I was looking for.

I looked through the papers first. The story was very familiar. His credit cards — and there were many of then — were maxed out. Designer label after designer label, boutiques in Bond Street getting some regular mentions. His school fees for three children were outstanding, figures in red on the latest ones and carrying a final notice. Renovations to the property, including the kitchen, were racking up interest fees that only added to the amounts owed.

I went to the filing cabinets. One of them contained a neatly-labelled folder for bank accounts. I withdrew it and took it over to the desk, sat down and begun to go back in time, newest to oldest. It confirmed the bleak picture of the credit card bills. Overdraft up to its limit. Then, bingo! Every month, there was a credit of ten thousand pounds — someone was spending money the moment that it was earned. With all the evidence against her, that was almost certainly Mrs Selby.

So, the question was, where were the regular credits coming from? I picked up the folder, the papers on his desk and the laptop for later examination and went downstairs. Or at least, that was my intention. The door to the master bedroom — biggest room, decorated in shades of pink, awakened my curiosity. I walked in and saw a vast collection of wall-to-wall wardrobes with mirrored fronts. I couldn't resist looking inside. I opened the first door, and the picture I had formed upstairs was corroborated: pair after pair of shoes neatly packed in their original boxes. Big collection of handbags, too. Racks and racks of clothes, including a pair of black leather leggings and top that looked like it formed part of an outfit for a dominatrix. The whole picture was obscene.

On entering the basement, I gave a nod to Palmer to say we could leave. 'Give Mrs Selby a receipt for the laptop, please, Jane,' he said, rising from the sofa. 'Stay as long as necessary. Any overtime will be covered. Not too many fags, eh, — shows the wrong example.'

We drove back to the Zeus building for me to pick up my car and he to catch up on the latest position. Once there, I placed the papers and laptop in the boot of the Beamer and signalled to Palmer that he should join me when he could.

Back in the office, I put the laptop and papers on the table and started sorting the papers into groups for easiest examination, category by category. The bank was of prime importance. If we could get details on the money paid in, we might be able to work back to their source. If we presumed the people behind the bombing — call him or her 'the drugs baron' — had one bank account, then there were two routes to follow — the payments from the casinos and the payments into Selby's account. The same account would be good; half the work needed. It would be sloppy on his/her part, but one had to hope — without hope, where would we be?

CHAPTER TEN

That evening, there would be four meetings: a gathering of Shannon Investigation Limited; Palmer next in importance; then Albert from Abacus; and a word with Dangerous, for a scheme I had in mind to test out a theory. I went to the room facing the river and made myself a stiff vodka and orange juice on a ton of ice and took a bit of time out to try to dissemble what was becoming a difficult and unclear picture. At exactly the right moment, Norman walked in. He helped himself to a cold beer and sat down with me — two sentimental men gazing at a scene of tranquillity.

'Getting complicated,' he said. 'We're dealing with the big boys now. What happened to Cherry brings more pressure on a pot that might boil over at any moment. We've been lucky so far — just a smashed windscreen and Cherry escaping a serious episode. It's not often I talk like the boss, but we need to know who will pursue the matter and who wants to bow out.'

'I've been thinking the same,' I said. 'Let's assemble everybody and see who is on which side, and whether we move on from here, or lick our wounds and bow out gracefully from the field of battle, if you don't mind mixed metaphors.'

Fifteen minutes and a refill of vodka later and we were all in the river room, including Valentine, who had been looking after Anji. Pep talk? No. I must be democratic.

'The situation is like this,' I said. 'Cherry is in hospital and doing well. One more day and she will be back with us. Lucky break. If Anji hadn't gone back for her phone, we would all have been caught up in the blast from the bomb. Thank you, Anji.'

She gave a small smile. Beryl poured her a glass of white wine out of gratitude — no, kinship. A group locked together by friendship and, hopefully, common purpose. Good versus evil. Putting the world to rights. David and Goliath. Size — resources — don't matter.

'We've got ourselves into something big,' I said. 'People who will kill wantonly to protect their ill-gotten gains. No doubt about it, this is a big decision. I know which way I would like to go forward, but I respect your views: this is not what you signed up for. There's no disgrace in saying, "stop now." Show me the way.'

Valentine put his hand up. 'I know I'm not officially part of the team, but I must say what I feel. I have never felt so included before. I have a purpose in life through you. You stand for something — something noble, if that is not too wet. It's people like you who make a difference. Don't give up, is what I would say.'

Anji went to stand next to Valentine, put her arms around him and kissed him on the cheek. 'This is a question about morals and whether we can be frightened into doing the immoral thing. I vote not to give up. *Illegitimi non carborundum*. Don't let the bastards grind you down.'

'Norman?' I said. 'You bankroll all this that we have. Without you, none of this would exist. Your opinion probably is the most important. How do you feel about this?'

'Hell of a rollercoaster ride,' he said. 'When you have a small business, the highs are higher and the lows are lower — never the middle ground. Business or personal hat on, I'm conflicted. Business hat, first. We've built up a big reputation around not being frightened by anything or taking the easy course: clients trust us to do the right thing. If it were to leak out that we gave in to pressure, then that reputation crashes and burns. We have to stick to our guns, or the business folds. With my personal hat on, I would hate to see harm come to any of you — death even, looking on the blackest side. It would be a responsibility from which I would never recover. I say go for it, but I'm an old man, not a youngster like Anji with her life ahead of her. Death means less to me. I respect, though, the views of those who want to go no further. Even if it's just Nick and I, we will not be intimidated. Let's see this through to the end and hold our heads high.'

'Arthur?' I said.

'I don't make eloquent speeches.'

'Eloquent is a good start,' I said.

'We go back a long way,' he said. 'True friends are hard to find. I don't let my friends down. End of speech.'

'Morag,' I said. 'Your turn next.'

'Like Arthur, I'm not used to being called to make speeches — twenty years with the police without ever being asked my opinion. I like it here,' she said. 'No, I love it here. I'd be lost without my role here. It gives me purpose. What would I do instead? I'd soon get bored with endless cruises with Norman, nice though that would be. No offence meant.'

'None taken,' Norman said.

She smiled at him. 'I stick by Norman's side. That's all I want to say.'

'Last and not least,' I said. 'Beryl?'

'I don't really deserve a vote,' she said. 'I've only been here five minutes.'

'Do you want to quit while you're ahead?' I said. 'No one would think any the less of you.'

'Like Arthur said, you don't let your friends down. Let's go for it.'

'*Nem con*, no one against,' I said, with a huge sigh of relief. 'Time to get on with planning our next moves, then. Notepad, someone.'

Beryl, accustomed to taking dictation any minute, produced one out of thin air. I scribbled a list down and passed it to her. 'Can you get these things done by Monday, please?'

She looked at the list and gazed at me with puzzlement.

'Questions later,' I said to her. 'You'll find the London Fog raincoat in the left-hand wardrobe. Morag, can you get twenty-two thousand pounds in cash — again by Monday morning. You'd better get us a safe, too. Can't be too careful with that much cash around. Pursue that with Norman. Fix up a meeting with Campion and Shapiro for four o'clock on Monday. Tell them it's an interim debrief. Can you get Abacus — of "you can count on us" fame — over here in an hour?'

'Consider it done,' she said.

I turned to Anji. 'There's a laptop on my office table. If it's not password protected, copy the contents on to the external hard disc, so that I can give it back to Palmer — we need to keep him onside. Arthur, a word, please. Scurry, everyone. Remember,' I said, 'time has no friends.'

'What does that mean?' said Arthur.

'I don't know,' I said. 'I just thought it sounded a good line to end on. Norman, if you can stay behind, I'd like your views on something.'

All bar Arthur and Norman went about their allotted tasks, leaving the three of us alone to plot.

'Arthur,' I said, 'what's your chances of recruiting ten people — they don't have to be men — who would like two hundred in cash for half an hour's work on Monday?'

'No problem,' he said. 'Cash in hand always goes down a treat.'

A thought struck me. 'They have to able to read and write.'

'You should have said that beforehand,' he said. Then he winked at me. 'Only joking, Nick. So good to wind you up now and again. Your face was a picture.'

'This is what they have to do.' I explained the plan to him.

He nodded his approval. 'Sounds fun,' he said.

'Till then, your job is to shadow us, Arthur.'

He nodded his head and left us to set about recruitment.

'What do you think?' I asked Norman. 'Will it work?'

'It's a gamble,' he said, 'but maybe that's the name of the game. We could always regard it as legitimate expenses if it goes belly up. No one loses at the end of the day, we could claim. Depends on your point of view, I suppose. What are our chances of getting ten per cent of any frauds found?'

'Campion is a bit niggardly about money — a miser, I think you could say — but I reckon he will see it as progress, even though it won't be a factor he considered in our contract. If he gets picky, I'll not press him. There's a lot of work still to be done at Zeus. Regard it as an investment, Norman.'

'What about this young lad Valentine,' he said. 'Anji seems struck by him. What do you see as his role?'

'Just to crunch some numbers with Anji — a whole host of them behind calculating the odds of what I think is a real fraud and enable us to identify the culprits.'

'Sounds like a lot of work to do,' Norman said. 'I'll leave you to get on with it. Don't forget I'm here if you need me. An old head is a wise head.'

The front door buzzer sounded. If it wasn't our so-called friend at Abacus an hour early, which I doubted, it must be Palmer.

He was still neat and tidy even after what must have been a hard day. I took him into the office. Anji and Valentine looked up from Selby's laptop.

'I suppose we could use first names,' I said to Palmer.

'I don't think so, Shannon,' he said. 'The name suits you. You're like a winding river in Ireland carving out its course, never knowing in which way you would go.'

'Gosh, that's profound.'

'There's no law that says police officers can't be profound.'

I suppose he was right. I'd never thought of that before. Prejudice strikes again.

'What progress, Anji?' I said.

'The good news is that it is not password protected. The bad news is that it is a hell of a jumble. Selby didn't seem to file anything. No folders. Most of the stuff just has a date in the file name. I think it's going to take the whole weekend to sort out. I've transferred it all to our external hard disk, like you said.'

'Then so be it,' I said. 'Tomorrow is Friday. I'll go back to Zeus and you can concentrate on crunching some numbers and I can carry out some interviews: if we can be at that point, it would be great. I'll pitch in, too. Valentine, can you look after the examination of the odds? We may have to narrow the search. Football is the next biggest revenue stream after horse racing. Concentrate on that. Anji, can you devote yourself to Selby's laptop? OK, guys. Time to quit for the day. Start afresh in the morning. Early would be good. And we mustn't forget Simpson. Any spare moment on him would be great.'

They both said 'Yes, chef' or whatever the equivalent was for a forensic accountant. I turned to Palmer. 'You can take the laptop away and give it to your forensic boys — we'll keep the papers for the moment. I doubt they'll do much with it till Monday, so we will still be ahead of the game.'

'This is not a game,' Palmer said. 'A person has been murdered.'

'Apologies. Bad choice of words. What I meant is that it is a race, a race to find the killer — or, one might better say, the person who paid the killer — before he or she covers their tracks. Our only chance is to follow the money trail. We've got three shots — the money paid into Selby's bank account, the money through betting shops and the same for the bank details from the casinos.'

'How much time do you need?' he said.

'Give me a week,' I said.

'No can do,' he said. 'Every day that goes by is a potential nail in my coffin. I'll give you till close of play on Wednesday — I'll take sick leave Monday and Tuesday, and then I'll have to pass everything upwards. Let my super decide who takes it over. Sigh of relief all round. Get shot of the bloody thing. Nest of vipers. All that stuff. Sorry, Shannon, but that's my final offer.'

'Beer to seal the deal?' I said.

'As I'm technically not on duty, then that would be good. Most hospitable.'

I walked through to the river room and got two beers from the fridge and popped the caps — didn't bother with glasses. Real men. Took them back into the office and handed one to Palmer. 'Have you got drip mats?' he said.

I'd forgot about his OCD. I went back to the river room and took two drip mats off the coffee table.

When I arrived back in the office, he was rolling the bottle on his forehead before taking a swig. 'You know,' he said, 'I've got three months to go before my retirement. I'd thought I'd be winding down. How wrong I was. You've been a game changer, if you pardon me using the *g* word after what I've said. First, the law firm murder, and now this. You do tend to complicate matters, Shannon.'

'You're not the first to say that. Won't be the last either, I suspect. What good clean fun we have together.'

'I wonder what my wife thinks of that as she places my dinner in the oven to spoil one more time.'

'I reckon she might wish for that when you've retired and are hanging around the house all day. You don't seem to be the type to play golf or bridge. No hobbies like stamp collecting.'

'Philately will get you nowhere,' he said with a smile. 'You've even got me cracking jokes. Wonders will never cease.'

* * *

After Palmer, all that was left for the day was Albert Archer of Abacus — you know the slogan. His hand shook as we went through the awkward greeting ritual. It felt clammy, too. I resisted wiping my hand on my trousers. Whatever was going through his mind, I had empathy for. This was all out of his comfort zone. A two-bit shoestring crossing horns with the big guys. I offered him a beer, which he declined. It was plain that he just wanted to say his piece, take the money for his work so far and get as far away from us as quickly as possible.

Then I remembered his penchant for whisky. I went back to the river room and picked up a bottle of single malt, some ice and two lowball glasses. He didn't say no this time: the pull of the malt was too great to resist. I put everything on the table and asked him to help himself. He poured himself a large measure neat, took a swig and smiled: I put some ice in my glass and a small amount of scotch for me, the ice designed to cut out any harshness, which shouldn't be there in a single malt. Whisky wasn't my spirit of choice, but I joined him to set a better mood for the conversation. Two buddies chewing the fat.

'This is getting out of hand,' he said. 'What should have been a simple act of following some people around and making notes has turned into a whole level higher. If I knew what a quantum leap was, I'd use that phrase. I said it before: I didn't sign up for this, for bombs and murder.'

'Look on the bright side. You've got one less person to follow. You're left with the three women. I don't see why there should be any threat from them. There's also now the new deadline. We won't be involved after the end of next week. Next Friday, it's finito. Hang up your gun and ride off into the sunset. Gone forever. You can lay back around the pool in some foreign land sipping scotch with the money you've earned.'

'Or I could be dead.'

'Don't be so melodramatic. What harm can come from a bit of shadowing the three daughters of Campion? They won't even know you're there. If you do your job well, that is.'

He finished his drink and poured another. I noticed his hand wasn't shaking anymore. Oh, the recuperative power of whisky!

'How's business?' I said. 'Can you afford to turn down a job of this size? More lucrative than following errant husbands cheating on their wives. Or vice versa.'

'The daily rate goes up from now,' he said. 'Let's call it danger money. Double from now on.'

I'd been prepared to go up even higher. He had me over a barrel, if he did but know it. I didn't know anyone else who could do the job, and I didn't have the time to start a new search from scratch. Arthur was too conspicuous for this kind of job, unfortunately.

I hesitated, making it seem as if he was pushing me past my limit.

'You drive a hard bargain, Archer,' I said. 'Daily rate doubled from tomorrow. Do the women in the order that's most convenient for you. I want daily updates from now on.'

We shook hands on the deal and finished our whiskies.

'Take the bottle,' I said. 'Show of good faith.'

He didn't need any second telling. Picked up the bottle and left me in peace to relax before a busy day tomorrow. I poured the remains of my scotch into the sink and splashed a large measure of vodka over some ice and sat with it, looking at the Thames following its lazy course down river. Norman walked into the room and poured himself a glass of red wine.

'Penny for them,' he said, sitting down opposite me.

'It's all got very complex,' I said. 'Very dangerous, too. We've all agreed to carry on. Took a vote on it. We all knew the risks. Cherry is an ever-present reminder of the stakes that people will go to and how lucky we have been so far. I don't want anyone else to die, anyone else on my conscience in the future.'

'*Nem con*, you said. So let's play it out, *nem con*,' Norman said. 'We may not be *The Magnificent Seven*, but we're a pretty good team. I'd hate to be pitched against us. Tell you what,' he said. 'Tomorrow I'll go through all the paperwork while Anji goes through Selby's computer; Valentine can go with you to Zeus and carry on working out the odds. Oh, and we'll check on Simpson, too. That leaves you free to do some more interviews. Does that sound like a plan?'

'Best we've got,' I said. 'Hell, let's go with it.'

'Cheers,' he said.

We clinked our glasses. The vodka tasted even better.

CHAPTER ELEVEN

On Friday morning, Valentine and I drove the Beamer to the Zeus complex. The guard routine was higher since the bomb. Not only were we and the boot searched, but the inside was subjected to a thorough going over. Horse bolted.

There were a lot of car park spaces: many staff must have parked up somewhere en route, hopped on the Docklands Light Railway and walked from the nearest station. One area had been cordoned off by the police and a tent put up to preserve the scene of the bombing and allow the forensic team to get on with their work. I did what the other drivers had done and parked as far away from the building as possible.

Once we were installed in our office, I sent Valentine off to arrange an interview with the football team of expert and watcher. I imagined that football would be a lucrative medium for fraud. Lots of ways to throw a game or key aspects of it: penalties missed; first yellow card; sending off; in play bets of many possibilities and so on. Time would tell.

Meanwhile, I looked over the calculations of profits generated or lost by each team. Too early to tell, but I was optimistic. I was sure that something was going on. It's that annoying itch you get and can't quite reach to scratch.

I was interrupted by a call from Morag. 'Are you alone?' she said.

'Just me here slaving over something or other.'

'I have had a call from Lady Livia. You will meet her for lunch tomorrow — not invited to lunch, but a direct order to attend. She said it was confidential. Stressed that no one, and that means no one, must find out. One o'clock at Le Grand Delice. Shall I tell her yes?'

'Seems too good an opportunity to turn down. Thanks, Morag. Better keep it to just you and me for the moment. See you later.'

I called Cherry while looking at the laptop. She sounded weary and downbeat: probably starved of interaction with some interesting people. And me, of course! I'm sure the staff were well intentioned, but there is a tendency to treat all patients patronisingly. I told her the latest of what had happened: the bomb — although she would have read some of the details in the morning papers and news programmes on the TV — our plan of action; the support for it by everyone. We would not be defeated. She perked up. I told her that I was missing her, how much I loved her and that I would visit her as soon as I could in the afternoon.

Valentine returned and told me I was on in an hour and that he would go out for some coffee meantime. I didn't say no. Good for both of us to be fuelled up for the morning.

It would seem that horse racing had made a slight loss, but that was to be expected due to limits on bets being made by the government, the greater need to economize in the current climate and the swings and roundabouts of fortune — sometimes the gods just have it in for you. Gaming machines made a loss; again the new rules for the maximum stake might account for that. I could see that the emphasis would decline along with the ultimate winding down of Betting Shops. Greyhound racing could be ruled out — it was a small income stream and wouldn't affect the overall figures. I had heard mumblings in the past about greyhound racing being fixed. Owners taking it in turn to win races and so on, but it was still small beer.

With the demise of Selby came a vacuum that had to be filled quickly. I didn't know which one of the sisters would take over, but my guess was Violet — she of the lesser ambition with the sights of Rose and Petunia being set higher. They would hold out for Head of Publishing and of Broadcasting. The takeover of Zeus had begun.

I had arranged to meet the football team in the cafeteria — our allocated office was too small, and Valentine could work there undisturbed. I also felt a more casual environment might bear a greater crop of fruit from the tree there when I shook it — less of the mood of an inquisition.

The cafeteria was more or less empty — too early for lunch, no demand for its watery coffee — and I spotted the team easily. They were sitting at a table by the window, and I hoped the view wouldn't distract them. We made introductions and got the interview underway.

The team comprised a man in his early thirties and a woman of similar age. The man was called Johnny Fenton — expert — and the woman was called Avril Walters — watcher. Walters stood out from the crowd, not for her mixed-race skin colour but a voluminous amount of jet-black hair in tightly packed curls. It hung down past her shoulders. This was a woman of supreme confidence, untamed by the system.

She was wearing a light blue denim jumpsuit with black high-heel peep-toe strappy sandals. She looked toned like she had a personal trainer at her every whim. She was wearing a sports watch in prominent show like she really wanted you to know that she was a fitness junkie. I wondered what her diet was like — vegan or vegetarian was my guess — be a shame for all that exercise to be blown by a bacon sandwich. She was sipping at a can of Red Bull.

Fenton was an ex-sportsman, I presumed, because he had the look of someone who had bloated and gone to fat. It happened to those who had at one time been very fit and then had to stop the exercise. There was a walking stick on the table in front of him.

He had blond hair cropped close and a short beard which was darker than his hair, which had me wondering what his natural colour was. There were lots of rings on his fingers and a flash watch — Rolex? — which might have been real. Might have.

'Can we start with some context?' I said, 'How did you get here?'

'Just walked up the stairs,' Fenton said.

What a card.

'Nice one,' I said, restraining myself. 'Tell me your history. What brought you to the positions you have today?'

'I'll start,' said Walters. 'I like talking about myself.'

As if Fenton didn't like the same, I thought.

'I got a media studies degree from what might be described as a second-tier concrete university, which led to a junior job on the football production team at the BBC. I wanted to be in front of the camera, but who doesn't? I worked hard — knew every stat going — but never got the opportunity. Their loss.' She took another sip of her drink. 'Been here five years now — my football knowledge impressed them at the interview. Got me six months' probation, and then took over when the previous occupant left for greener pastures. I'm happy where I am now. I don't intend to move, although the Selby replacement is an unknown factor.'

'So what makes you happy?' I said.

'Being, basically, my own boss. The chance to be around some heroes in the footballing word. Glamour, I suppose. It's a great way to spend your working hours. Johnny and I fit well together. Nice environment — be different without Johnny.'

'And you, Johnny? Feel the same? The chemistry works for you?'

'I couldn't wish for a better partner,' he said. 'We share the same hopes and dreams.'

'Which are?'

'To live in the style to which we aspire. Champagne, oysters and Wagyu beef,' he said. 'To still be a part of our beloved game.'

'And your background?' I said.

'Council house kid,' he said. 'I went to Loughborough. You know about it?'

'Sporty is all I know.'

'It's not just about that. Fine university as well. I was taking a business degree. I joined the football team and realised I had a talent for it — I'd only played a bit at school. Got better with every game I played. Had some trials with some big teams. About to sign for Chelsea and then got my leg broken by a bad tackle. They had to put plates and screws in it. I had a four-month layoff. Started training again, and then it got broken a second time. I had to come to the realisation that I could never play football again.'

'Must have been hard,' I said.

'Devastating. But you have to move on from there, or you start doubting yourself and give up. I'd built up a lot of contacts in the footballing world. This job came up, and it seemed like a big opportunity to use those contacts and be a part of a world I'd come to love.'

'And they all lived happy ever after,' I said.

Fenton looked at me with loathing, as if I was some sort of lowlife, some sort of threat to him like a bacterium, and had to be disposed of at the earliest opportunity. What had I done? Too flippant? Probably. Whatever, I doubted I would get much more out of them.

'How much,' I said, 'do you — what's the word, interfere, no — *intervene* between gambler and computer?'

'All the time,' Walters said. 'Do you think they will have created these full-time jobs if they were not required to be used all day? We wouldn't be here now if it was not true.'

'So,' I said, 'how much is based on your contacts and how much gut feel?'

'You have to realize that there are a whole host of matches throughout the world that you can bet on. It's impossible to

106

know them intimately. We let the computer decide on those, and, anyhow, they're chicken-feed bets — we take very few bets on those matches so they're hardly going to make much difference to the bottom line. Avril and I cover the bigger leagues — Premier League, Championship, Leagues One and Two. That's where the big money bets take place. That's where we make our profits.'

'I understand,' I said, 'that profits are down this year. That's why we're here. Any thoughts about that?'

'Just the run of the ball,' Fenton said. 'Everyone can have a bad run sometimes. Can't legislate for it. It'll turn round.'

'Maybe your contacts have been listening to the wrong gossip,' I said. 'Were less useful to you? Been counterproductive, even.'

'Like I said,' Fenton said, 'it's just the run of the ball. It's like your star striker missing an open goal. He'll score next time.'

I wondered whether all his metaphors were football-based. One-track mind?

'How many times have you, Avril, not agreed to one of Johnny's suggestions? How many have you countermanded?'

'It doesn't work that way,' she said. 'We work together, analysing everything, rather than Johnny proposing and me assessing.'

'Sounds a little cosy,' I said. 'How many times do you both disagree? Or how many times do you, Johnny, just function as a rubber stamp?'

'Nothing wrong with cosy,' Fenton said. 'We function as a team, exactly how decisions should be made. Be a rotten life if we always disagreed. What would be the point?'

'I thought that was exactly the point,' I said. 'Questioning the decision before the final odds were decided?'

'I don't like the way this conversation is going,' Fenton said.

'I'm sorry that you feel that way,' I said. 'I didn't mean to imply anything. Part of my job is to search for holes in the system — to sort out the good and the bad. It could be that you two turn out to be the exemplar as to how a team should function. You might get some Brownie points from it.'

'Maybe I was too hasty,' he said. 'You can see how your questions looked. Seemed like you were trying to dig some dirt on us.'

'God forbid,' I said. 'Last thing on my mind. Especially in the current circumstances. Do you have any ideas as to why someone would want to kill Selby? Anyone have grudges against him?'

'I'd put it down to sabotage,' said Walters. 'There must still be lots of people looking for revenge against Zeus for moving the print works here and the host of workers made redundant as a consequence of that.'

'But why Selby?' I said. 'Surely if someone was to plant a bomb it would be Campion or Shapiro that would be the target. Get much more publicity that way. Selby seems an odd choice.'

'Maybe it's just the luck of the draw,' said Walters. 'Whoever did it just wanted any car, and Selby's was in the wrong place at the wrong time.'

'You could be right,' I said. 'How was he viewed by the staff? A good boss? Bully? Prejudiced? What do you think, Johnny?'

'Don't talk ill of the dead, Johnny,' said Walters.

'Why not?' he said. 'Shannon wants to know the truth. Can't do any harm now.'

'Sounds like that is an avenue I should pursue,' I said. 'Tell me more.'

'To be frank,' Johnny said, 'he was hopeless. Fish out of water. Why they ever moved him from Publishing I have no idea. He just didn't understand the world of Gambling. How he spent his day was beyond me. He pretty much left everybody to their own devices. Perhaps that was a deliberate management style. To me, it didn't seem to make much sense. The Division won't miss him. We're not going to be in a vacuum, not rudderless.'

'Let's leave him to rest in peace,' said Walters.

'Was he unpopular with the staff?' I said, ignoring her. 'Did they all feel the same as you?'

'Probably,' Fenton said. 'For someone who liked to get their heads down and get on with their work, he was manna sent from heaven.'

'Look,' said Walters, 'I really must get on with things. For now, that's it.'

She stood up from the table. Fenton did the same, using his stick for balance. We shook hands and I was left staring out of the window trying to make sense of things. I didn't like either of them — Walters for the chip on her shoulder because of not making it in front of the camera, Fenton for the impression that the world owed him a living because of his injury — I told myself not to be influenced by that, but it was hard.

When I arrived back at our allotted office, Valentine was getting indigestion from crunching data. 'How's it going?' I said.

'Slow,' he replied. 'You wouldn't believe how many bets there are in football. I'm still on the first month. How was the football team?'

'Dire,' I said. 'A narcissist and a wide boy. Oh, how I hope they've done something bad.'

'Message came through that you have to see Violet as soon as possible.'

'Any more detail?'

'Just said it was urgent. Her office.'

'Are you happy to keep going here if I go now?'

'Wouldn't mind a break, but I best keep going.'

'See you later then.'

I went across to Violet's office and knocked on the door. No answer. I tried again. Still no answer.'

A voice rang out behind me.

'You won't find her there,' a man said. 'You'll find her in Selby's old office. Been promoted to replace him.'

My god, she didn't waste any time. I was obviously behind everybody on the news. Wasn't on the email circulation list as well as Christmas cards. Violet Head of Division. What would change, was the key question? New boss just like the old boss, as the song went? Not where Selby was involved. Not a good example to follow. Out with old and in with the new would be the mantra.

I knocked on the door of the new office. A curt voice shouted 'Enter'.

Inside was a case of not wasting any time. Her modern prints already hung on the walls. There was a large cardboard box in one corner which I took to be Selby's contents. Violet looked at me and waved her hand at a chair. I sat down and looked at her. Same eye shadow above those electric-blue eyes, same heavy mascara. All the same except for the smug look.

'I take it celebrations are in order,' I said. 'Congratulations. Does a new broom sweep clean?'

'In your case, yes,' she said. 'I'm not happy with the way you work. I've had complaints from my staff,' Presumably Fenton and Walters, 'about you being disruptive. Taking too much of their time. They also do not like your attitude. Aggressive, they say. Pointing fingers at them where there is no evidence of wrongdoing. Making accusations without any foundation. What do you say about all that?'

'It would seem that the wrong interpretation has been placed on my methods. I apologize for that, but I was charged by Sir Gerald and David Shapiro to investigate the Gambling Division. I can't do that on figures alone. I need to talk to people — get the facts direct from the horse's mouth. I try to be as non-disruptive as I can.'

'Well, it hasn't been happening. My staff have been made to think they are under a cloud of suspicion. I'm suspending your access to my staff — all dedicated people — from today. You will trouble us no more.'

'I have an interim debrief with Sir Gerald and David Shapiro on Monday afternoon. We will see then what I am permitted to do. I suspect there will no bounds on our work. I look forward to seeing you Tuesday morning. I suspect it will not be the sort of issue that you would like when talking about a new job with new responsibilities. Are you sticking with your position, or would you like to reconsider your current decision?'

'You can't frighten me by playing the Sir Gerald and David Shapiro cards. You know who I am. Your interference is costing money and morale by the time and the stance you have taken. That is what counts. Pack your bags, Shannon.'

'I won't give you the stock reply of *you have not heard the last of which*, but you have put yourself in a perilous position. See you Tuesday.'

I stormed out of the room with all the dignity I could summon up. I may have temporarily lost the battle, but not the war. Pyrrhic victory for her. Violet would come to regret this.

* * *

I walked out to get some fresh air. I wished I smoked. Something which might have cleansed my mind. I was rattled and needed some outlet. I saw Arthur's white van parked among the host of private cars. There was Valentine's Beetle Cabriolet, too. What a puzzle he was. So underrated. There was untapped potential in the lad which would never be fulfilled if he tried to follow in his father's footsteps. Life would always be awkward for him.

I walked back inside. Valentine was still hunched over the laptop. 'How's it going?' I said. 'Any progress?'

'Needle in a haystack,' he said.

'Do we still have remote access to the Zeus system?'

'No change as far as I can tell,' he said.

'Then let's pack up and head home. We're not welcome anymore.'

'If we ever were,' he said.

'Amen.'

CHAPTER TWELVE

Before we left, I called Arthur on his mobile and informed him about the change of plan. Told him to follow Valentine back and then we could all meet up and reappraise things. I began to have doubts about the balance of power regarding Sir Gerald and his stepdaughter. Would she prevail — would her mother prevail, more to the question? — and get us off the job? Maybe Shapiro would be a mediator and get us a stay of execution. I didn't like giving up on something, especially where we had done so much. I felt that we were close to a breakthrough, if only given a chance.

Once back, I got everyone together around the office table and informed them of Violet's show of power, and that she might outrank us when she spoke to Sir Gerald. There was a general mood of despondency among us that needed to be assuaged if we were to turn a corner and make progress.

'Arthur,' I said first. 'We're stretched. I can't give Albert from Abacus any more to do, and we need to get some background information about two more people. You're too conspicuous — no offence . . .'

'None taken.'

'. . . too easy to spot on foot, should I say? Keeping to your van, take a look at where these two people live and see if anything jumps out at you. Are you happy to do that?'

'No problem,' he said. 'Just give me the details and I'll start straight away. Do you still want me to shadow you guys?'

'I suspect we won't be going anywhere for a while. I'll visit Cherry later, but I can do that solo. Morag, Beryl, are the plans all ready for Monday?'

'The safe will be fitted this afternoon,' Morag said. 'I've already got the cash from the bank — I must admit I felt a bit nervous on the way back, even though I had Beryl for company.'

'Everything else on the list is ready,' said Beryl.

'Then I think you both can stand down. Coffee would be good, if you don't mind.'

They left the room and I looked around the table: Norman had a stack of paper in front of him; Anji had her laptop; Valentine was writing out names, addresses and car details of Fenton and Walters for Arthur. He passed them across the table and Arthur left.

'Norman,' I said. 'Let's start with you. Anything interesting from Selby's papers?'

'Mostly confirms what we know already. He was in a bad financial mess. I didn't know school fees could be so high. Three kids at around six grand a term each — after tax, too — soon mounts up. I hope they're worth it and that it's not money straight down the drain. There was one thing, though. I'm not sure that it's pertinent, but here goes. There were a couple of notes on memo paper in what I presume was his handwriting of a reference to "the syndicate". Both had a question mark after them. It may be nothing, but it sounds fishy to me. I know you can have a syndicate to own a racehorse, but how that fits in, I don't know.'

'Anji,' I said, 'anything from his computer?'

'I don't think we could say that he didn't know what a mess he was in. There was an attempt to analyse the position through a spreadsheet of monthly outgoings, but it didn't come to anything. Didn't change behaviour, didn't want the truth. I don't think he could do anything about his wife. She called the shots, he was hen-pecked, although the Americans have a more direct phrase for it. She shows no intent to let up on her spending. It made him ripe for something criminal, blackmail possibly, bribes is another reason. He did take steps to check out a remortgage on the house, but that was declined. The bank statements show the unexplained credit each month. I go with Norman. My guess is he was paid for something illegal. There's a scam going on somewhere.'

'Valentine,' I said, 'last but no means least. Are we any closer in finding out which team was responsible for the most losing bets?'

'It's a slow grind,' he said. 'I really can't say how long it might take.'

'I can't help but think that we're missing something here,' I said. 'What do you always say, Norman? What's your favourite saying?'

'It's all about the cash,' he said.

'What if we start at the other end,' I said. 'Where are the ill-gotten gains going? There must be information on payments going into user accounts. What if we search for big credits on the accounts data? There can't be many people, surely, that make big regular profits.'

'Sounds like a plan,' Norman said. 'Nothing better to do.'

Beryl came in with the coffee and the mood lightened. We knew what we were doing now. We had a purpose. Long may it last.

* * *

Cherry wasn't in a good mood. 'They're keeping me in till Monday, and I'm sick of this place already.'

Our friendly nurse walked by and I called to her. She came over and saw Cherry's face. She prepared herself for a possible argument.

'Cherry says you're keeping her in till Monday,' I said. 'Is there a problem?'

'The consultant is asking for more tests. Cherry isn't making the progress he had hoped. She's still complaining of headaches. The consultant wants an MRI scan. There's a backlog at the moment and the weekend coming up, so we're down on staff. We've scheduled a scan on Monday. If the results are good — no worrying signs — then she can go home in the afternoon. Please don't worry unduly.'

The nurse walked away. I could tell that Cherry was disappointed and close to tears. I felt her pain. It's so easy when in hospital to feel hopeless against the system. I felt just like a cog in something turning.

I placed the bag I had brought and started to unpack it. It wasn't one of the things she had asked for, but the miniature bottle of white wine packed in ice seemed to be a good pick-me-up. I poured it into the tumbler I had brought and then unwrapped the pyjamas and face creams and other esoterica that she had requested. I handed over a bunch of grapes that was not on her list. There was something about grapes and hospitals that meant you had to buy some on impulse.

While she packed everything away, I filled her in on the happenings since I had visited the day before.

'I'm sure everything will work out fine,' she said. 'You seem to have it all under control, all the angles covered,' she said. 'You just need that one breakthrough and it will all slot into place. I have a good feeling for this.'

We talked about Violet's show of power, her flexing of her muscles, and the change of attitude to us after her promotion and my thoughts on what I could do to get the ban lifted. Cherry was confident that my plan for Monday would do the trick.

'You're going to have to trust me on this one. I'm going to have lunch with someone. I promised not to tell anyone — a confidential meeting. If I tell you about the lunch date, I would be breaking my word.'

'Which you don't like doing,' Cherry said. 'An honour code.'

'But I didn't promise that person not to disclose the contents of that meeting, so I'll tell you all about it after the event.'

'It's a fine distinction to make,' she said. 'Bit of a weasel really, but I'll trust you.'

We went back to more news. I made her smile when talking about how the feisty Anji had morphed into a love-sick teenager who was putty in Valentine's hands. It was a situation that could be a problem if he had no feelings for her, but we would cross that bridge if it came to it. Cherry said that she would jump in, if necessary, with some maternal advice. First love can be so overpowering and its effects can last well into the future. I'd hate to see Anji hurt in any way. On the other hand, the attraction might be mutual. I liked the boy, and I felt he would treat her well.

I told her how much I missed her and that I would pick her up after what I hoped would be a productive meeting with Sir Gerald and Shapiro. I kissed her on the lips and left before melancholy broke like a wave over me. Roll on Monday and a celebratory bottle of champagne.

Back at the ranch, so they say, everyone was hard at work. I felt I wasn't pulling my weight, and that I had to do my bit.

'It seems like we will be working all weekend,' I said to Anji and Valentine. 'Why don't you guys take the evening off. Get a taxi to Canary Wharf and have dinner. There's plenty of choice there to meet all your desires. Get a taxi back, too. No walking unguarded without Arthur there to protect you. All on expenses, so indulge yourself.'

Anji didn't need a second offer and dropped what she doing to get herself ready. I sensed another little black dress coming. Fingers crossed for young love.

I poured myself a large vodka, this time with ice, tonic and lemon for a change and to up my rebel rating, and set to work where Valentine had left off. I was an hour in when I found it. I had identified the transactions where the money from the betting fraud went. And which team was responsible.

Eureka.

I went back to where Valentine had got and made it look like I hadn't done anything. Time to be silent. Let the winner take the spoils he deserved.

* * *

I was still sitting in the river room, taking slow sips of my vodka when they arrived back. My paternalism seemed to be increasing by the day.

Anji had on the strapless version of her infinite range of little black dresses. If ever there was a world shortage of little black dresses, Anji could release some of her stock. She had teamed it with her favourite black over-the-knee biker boots. A plain gold necklace with a heart on was her only accessory. Valentine had on a grey suit with a thin blue line running through, blue shirt, no tie.

They were holding hands.

Anji looked at me imploringly.

I nodded my head.

She smiled.

CHAPTER THIRTEEN

Le Grand Delice was a popular restaurant. It catered primarily for ladies who lunch — a white-of-egg omelette was their signature dish. Portions were small, but elaborately presented. They said that they tried to source locally, but that was a small part of their many exotic ingredients that had been flown halfway round the world. As I sat down, I wished I'd had a bigger breakfast.

The décor was basically shades of pink for tablecloths and napkins and a single pink rose in a tiny pink vase on each table. The rose was plastic. The walls were the lightest shade of pink and ceiling fans were whirling around for atmosphere as the room was air-conditioned. Lady Livia was fashionably late; ten minutes to be precise. She was wearing a long flowing dress in a Caribbean print — hummingbirds, primarily — and flat bejewelled sandals. Were the jewels real, I wondered? Her make-up was immaculate — applied by her maid? Her face was still frozen like a death mask, a tribute to work done by her plastic surgeon, if you like that kind of thing. I rose to meet her — no handshake or kisses on the cheek. The waiter pulled her chair out and helped her to sit comfortably. He gave us menus and asked for our drinks order. Livia asked for a spritzer and I ordered a vodka and orange juice — creature of habit — plus the fact that I wasn't driving — I had walked and caught the DLR and the tube. I had a feeling that alcohol might be the only pleasure from the lunch. I looked at the menus and was shocked by the prices (and was I supposed to pay?) and the fact was that there was really nothing I fancied. In the end, I chose turbot with ribbons of this and a jus of that, plus a sprig of some random herb as garnish. It was a creative dish that was totally uninspiring. Livia ordered her usual, whatever that turned out to be (spoiler alert — a tiny piece of tuna, cooked pink, of course — was there no getting away from pink? — with a mixed salad including edible flowers).

'My daughters don't seem to like you much,' Lady Livia said, after our plates were cleared and the waiter had used a miniature brush and pan to run over the table to gather up non-existent crumbs. 'They find you arrogant and disruptive and guilty of making unfounded accusations. In summary, they don't like your attitude. What do you have to say about that, Shannon?'

'I would say they are being oversensitive. You can't make an omelette — even a white one — without breaking eggs. Look on the positive side. By the end of the week I will be gone. If I'm allowed to continue, that is. Violet has made her position clear. She wants me out now and has created an awkward situation. Do I start running to Daddy?'

'As you say, awkward. I can usually handle Campion — in general, he goes along with what I say. Where you are concerned, though, Shannon, he seems to have a blind spot, resistant to my will. He likes the way you stand up to him. You wouldn't believe how many times he has told me about giving you five minutes and you only needed one. Don't present him with a dilemma — to choose between family or you. I would ask you to terminate your contract with Zeus before you do anything to make the situation worse.'

'I can't do that,' I said. 'I took on a job and I'm committed to finishing it. To walk away now would be to break my word. It would be without honour.'

'What is it with your sort of men that they talk about honour? Honour never put bread on the table or wine in your glass.'

'But with honour, you can look at yourself in the mirror and feel proud. You have self-respect and you're ready to meet your maker knowing you have done the right thing. Women can have honour, too. Do your daughters have honour?'

She let out an exasperated sigh. 'It should be me talking of honour — an old-fashioned concept — not you. Honour will hold you back in business. See sense and quit now.'

'Paradoxically,' I said, 'our business thrives through honour. We can be trusted to keep our word and keep our standards. We are one of one in a niche of the market. And, anyway, why the rush? Why was Violet promoted to Selby's job so rapidly, before what remains of him are yet in the ground? Why stress about us spending a few more days?'

'I have a plan for Zeus and my daughters' place in it. The plan must go ahead and must do so quickly.'

'I repeat what I said earlier. Why the rush?'

'Because Campion has cancer. He may not have long to live.'

As big a bombshell as that which had consumed Selby. I was shocked and sad in equal measures. 'Tell me all about it?' I said.

'Lung cancer — those filthy cigars he smokes.'

'Is there nothing that can be done?'

'Yes,' she said, 'if only he would listen. He could have the tumour removed and start chemotherapy and radiotherapy. He might squeeze a few more years out of it in that case. But, again, he is resistant. He doesn't want to live life in the shadow of his former self. He wants palliative care only. Six months and he's probably gone. Now do you understand the need to be swift?'

'So is the plan that before Sir Gerald's death your three daughters will head up all three divisions?'

'Exactly,' she said.

'And, after that, one will replace Shapiro?'

'Given decent time, that will be the case. Zeus will be ours.'

'Who else knows about the cancer?' I asked.

'Shapiro and my three daughters,' she said. 'Campion doesn't want anyone to learn about it until it gets obvious. He's going to try to soldier through until the last possible moment. Now, Shannon, will you stop?'

'No,' I said. 'If Sir Gerald doesn't want anyone to know, then that must be how I act.'

She slapped my face, threw her napkin on to the table and stormed out.

The things you do for honour.

And she did leave me with the bill.

CHAPTER FOURTEEN

Arthur arrived about ten on Sunday morning. There was a big smile on his face. 'You're going to love this,' he said.

'What will I love?' I said. 'Don't keep me in suspense.'

'Hear, hear,' said Anji.

'This Fenton guy,' he said. 'I got a good look at him when he got into his car at Zeus. Car was an ageing Renault Megane. It said short of cash. Didn't have the money to buy something more modern. Innocent as the day is long. I followed him to his gaff. He has an expensive flat at the Barbican. Very sought after. Big flats — apartments, they'd say — central London. Handy for the tube.'

'Agree,' I said. 'What next?'

'He parks up the car, goes upstairs and I start thinking what to do. Should I stay or move on to the Walters woman? I decided to stick around for a while. Half an hour later he comes out. Driving a Porsche with the top down. I can see him clearly. No mistake. We got him.'

'Well done, Arthur,' I said.

'There's more,' he said. 'I mosey on down to where the woman lives. Nice pad in Battersea. Terraced house. Old style. The type with Victorian features being put back in where the previous occupants had taken them out. Upmarket.

Drives a white Mini Cooper. Same as in *The Italian Job*. Vroom, vroom.'

'And?'

'I spot it in the parking area,' he said. 'Slap bang next to Fenton's Porsche.'

'Ah ha!'

'One last thing,' he said. 'There's a For Sale board outside her place. I got to wondering whether she's upsizing. Ill-gotten gains, maybe?'

'You're a gem, Arthur,' I said. 'Rough diamond, but still a diamond.'

'Where next?' he said.

'Cherry would love to get a visit from you. Mission of mercy. She's a bit down at the moment. You would cheer her up. After that, back here in case we need protection.'

'You got it,' he said. 'See you later.'

Anji blew him a kiss. How happy she was this morning.

I was expecting a visit from Archer of Abacus with a progress report, but he'd yet to show. Might have had a late night on the job. I gave him the benefit of the doubt. I looked at my watch and then over to where Valentine was wading through the gambling accounts. He should be there soon.

I made a coffee and sat in the river room waiting.

'Got it!' Valentine shouted. 'I've bloody got it.'

I looked at my watch again. Ninety minutes. Not bad for a tyro.

'Tell me all,' I said.

'Yes,' said Anji. 'Tell us all. Must be good news. I'm so excited.'

'You were right,' he said to me. 'It's football. There's an account that has more success even allowing for a lucky streak. Regular wins, although there are losses, too, but not many. Large stakes.'

'How much are we talking about?' I said.

'I've been back three months,' he said. 'Net winnings two hundred thousand pounds. God knows what we're talking about on an annual basis.'

'The name of this account?' I asked.

'Just down as "Prometheus".'

'The Greek mythology character who stole fire from the gods and gave it to mankind,' I said. 'The gods punished him by staking him out and letting the crows eat his liver every night. The liver regenerated in the day so that the punishment was endless.'

Anji raised an eyebrow. 'Just like the note Norman found in Selby's papers, the syndicate. Do you think Selby knew about this?'

'Almost certainly,' I said. 'I think he wanted a cut of the scam. Was using blackmail for him to take a slice of the action.'

'And that led someone to kill him?' Valentine asked.

'There's no limit to what someone will go to for money,' I said. 'We now need to assemble all the facts. Get compelling evidence on what's been happening. We need to find out where the winnings go. Identify a bank account, if possible. Trace it back from there. The job's far from done, but thanks to Valentine and everybody's hard work we have the breakthrough we needed. Check with Companies House and see if you can find out the directors. Norman will show you how. I know you've already done this,' I said to Anji, 'but regard it as a reminder. Valentine needs to learn.'

'How are they managing to defraud so much money?' Anji asked.

Time to air my theory.

'We know how the gambling operations make their money — it's down to their margin on every bet. In the long run, you can't beat the bookie. What if, however, someone turns that margin on its head? Fenton and Walters, for surely it is them, quote better odds than justified. They overrule the computer. Push up the odds in the syndicate's favour, say six to one instead of four to one — nothing too showy. Don't forget they have all the vital information in their heads to pick a surefire winner. Stake ten grand and at 6/1 you rack up sixty grand — bank half of it, say, and the rest on another 6/1. The money racks up rapidly. In the long run, the syndicate wins. Everyone involved makes money at the expense of Zeus. Easy when you come to think of it.'

I went through from my office to the river room and took three cold beers from the fridge — it was twelve o'clock, over the yardarm somewhere, I said to myself for justification — popped the caps, went back into the office and passed one each to Anji and Valentine.

'Congratulations, guys,' I said. 'Now we have to fill in the gaps and build a case. A big slog still to do, but we will get there in the end.'

'Are you going to tell Sir Gerald and Valentine's father what's going on at your meeting on Monday?' Anji asked.

'I doubt that we will be ready by then. Anyway, I love the drama we should have at the Friday meeting. I don't want anything to be a distraction. I want to remind you, too, that we are on a bonus of ten per cent of any fraud found. Go back a year and detail every transaction. Add them all up. This is looking like bonanza time. Added to that, we still have the money laundering to finalize. We need to track back on this guy Simpson and find where his money goes. Anji, can you try to get some information and identify a bank account? Then work forward by stages to the end user.' I passed her the business card that Simpson gave me and the details Valentine had got from the cashier. 'Keep working and we'll convene later. Meanwhile, slog away.'

I went into the river room and watched one of the pleasure boats that took the tourists for a ride — literally? — glide majestically by. This afternoon, I would visit Cherry and give her a progress report. I told myself she would soon be home. I missed her so much.

* * *

Archer came to prevent me feeling melancholy. Strange. There were sufficient good things to stop me feeling low.

He was wearing what used to be called 'mufti' by Norman. Pair of black slacks — not chinos — and a polo shirt in white. He didn't look seedy enough today to be a private eye, though there were bags under his bloodshot eyes. His hands shook a little till he had a gulp of the scotch I handed him from the new bottle. There but for fortune. I pledged myself I wouldn't have a vodka before sundown — didn't specify the country.

Archer sat down on one of the chairs facing my desk. I put the whisky bottle to his right.

'Mixed,' he said. 'Progress mixed.'

'Tell me about it,' I said.

'I started with the Violet bird. Pad down in Hammersmith. Nice area. Good for schools if you don't have the funds for the private ones. Big house — probably six bedrooms from what I could tell from the number of windows outside. Gothic-style, which in my book means ugly. Pillars either side of the front porch to give it a touch of class, but nothing seemed to match. What do they care? Must be worth a fortune.'

He picked up his scotch and took a long pull. He almost smiled.

'Yesterday they were throwing a party,' he said.

'It fits,' I said. 'Celebrating a promotion. What are the vibes?'

'Noisy, but the neighbours are far enough away not to be too bothered. Fireworks at nine — just about permissible. Visitors are in expensive cars. No one brings a bottle. Probably wouldn't have been good enough if they did. The whole shebang screams money. Money, money, money. They wrote a song about it.'

'Sounds like the sort of lifestyle one would expect from her job and from her family. Anything else?'

'Saw the two sisters. One looked like she wouldn't have been out of place hanging around street corners in the backstreets of Paddington. The other more chic — long flowing dress in summer colours. Got more class.'

'Anything more on the other two sisters?' I said. 'Anything we can use?'

'Depends what you want to use it for,' he said. 'I'm sensing you don't like them much. Would like something to use against them. Am I correct?'

'Seems like I have to work on my poker face,' I said.

'I left the party after the fireworks. Drove down to Islington to the tart's place. Sort of area where you have to be a politician to have a house there. Not all about money. More like being simpatico with your neighbours, if you know what I mean.'

'Exactly. Sounds like you don't like her either.'

'Pure envy,' he said. 'What a lifestyle when your biggest worry is whether the au pair is vegetarian or vegan when you're ordering your weekly shop from Waitrose.'

I nodded. He was good. Had a fine judgement of people. He may be a weasel, but a good weasel.

'As my last call of the day, I went to Petunia's place. Again, nice area — Brentwood in Essex. Big houses, green fields close by where you could walk the dog. The only drawback is that it's a long commute. Good trains into London, but I suspect she travels by car — likes her independence. Keep away from the masses. No mingling. The house backs on to a golf course. Modern detached, built around the turn of the century, by the look of it. The time when space was affordable.'

'Anything else?' I asked.

'If it's of any relevance, she's a smoker — might be a factor of why she's so thin. I like a broad with a bit of flesh on her. Came out of the front door, lit up and stood outside for a while savouring the hit from the nicotine. I did wonder whether the three of them were using something with a bit more of a kick. They're the sort of people who might have a man turn up at a party and deliver something to share among the guests. *Très chic.*'

I leaned back in my chair and stared at the ceiling to digest Archer's information and for a slice of inspiration.

'What do you want me to do next?' he said.

'I wish I knew.'

CHAPTER FIFTEEN

Sunday. A day of rest and relaxation for most. Just another day in the week for us. We were all working at building the cases against our suspects. And — would you believe it? — DI Palmer came round. He tossed a copy of *The Sunday Times* on my desk and sat in my client chair.

'Listen and learn,' I said to Anji and Valentine, who were hunched around the table in my office. It had to be something important to drag Palmer away from the gardening, rearranging the runner beans so that they were all completely vertical.

'Have you read the papers?' he said.

'I gave up reading the Sunday papers when they destroyed a rainforest to print every copy.'

'Business section, page five.'

I picked out the business section from the other four tons of paper and turned to the page he'd said. There in a short column was a picture of Petunia. The headline read, 'Ferguson suspended'. Ferguson, so it seemed, was Head of the Publishing Division at Zeus. There had been allegations of sexual misconduct against him. His suspension, the company said, was to allow a full internal review of the accusations and for the police, in parallel, to see if there was

128

any truth in them. And the relevant part? The bit that had brought Palmer round? He was to be replaced by Petunia Campion.

'Now the *Style* magazine,' he said. 'Bear in mind that, so I'm assured by my wife, because it is all in colour, the magazine is finalized three months in advance of publication — it's not up to date. Page nineteen is the bit that will interest you.'

The feature ran over four pages. The three sisters lauded for their key roles in the Zeus empire. Lots of advice on how to make it to the top in what is still a man's world. What to wear, illustrated by photos of the three sisters in their chosen power-dressed outfits and what make-up to use — cue close up of Casinov's vivid blue eyes. Fame at last.

'The master plan, the succession plan, is almost in sight,' I said. 'Violet Head of Gambling, Petunia Head of Publishing. Only Rose to go. I wonder what stunt they will pull for her to be Head of Broadcasting. And then, how long before one of the three replaces Shapiro?'

'Any coffee?' he said.

'Just what we need,' I said.

'I'll get it.' said Anji. 'We need a coffee break. My eyes are spinning.'

'Espresso with two sugars, please,' said Palmer. 'No, make that three.'

'And drip mats,' I added. 'What are we going to do?'

'What's with the *we*,' he said. 'I don't have anything against them. They've not done anything illegal. It's you who wants to see them fall from grace.'

'OK. Granted. Nothing illegal that we've found so far, but it leaves a nasty taste in my mouth.'

Anji brought in the coffees and placed them in front of us. His coffee looked like he could just about permit a stir after the amount of sugar in it.

'What progress your side?' I said.

'You first,' he said, 'then my reply will take it into account after how useful your report is.'

'I've got two people who have been pulling a scam that goes back — Anji, how long has the football fraud been going on?' I said.

'We've gone back a year, and it started then. Haven't checked previous years. Seemed like overkill,' she said.

'So it looks like at least a year,' I said. 'I wouldn't have thought much more than that as surely someone might have picked it up, although seeing the management today they may have not noticed. We'll hand over all our working papers to the Fraud Squad, or does it suit you better for you to?'

'You do it,' he said. 'Might get you a team bonus point if you need it after Cherry's long stint there. I'll send an accompanying note to say it was my idea to investigate. Let me know how you did it.'

'Of more interest to you,' I said, 'are scams in the casinos and Betting Shops that are a hotbed of money laundering. What would you like me to do with those?'

'I'll progress those,' he said. 'Again, tell me how you did it. I'll let you know who best to send it to. It crosses boundaries between departments. It needs some working out.'

'The only lead we have there is a guy called Simpson, gambles ten grand every night at the casino in Lakeside. You should pull him in. He might spill the beans on the big boys. The risk is that if we can't build a case, then alarm bells will ring and operations will shut down and be moved elsewhere and we have to start again from scratch. We have account details of where the money is going and we're trying to see where it moves on from there.

'So we're left with the bomb,' I continued. 'I suspect it's linked to the money laundering — bottomless pit for whatever they want to do. Even murder.'

'OK,' he said. 'Progress my side. The Bomb Squad have confirmed that it was a rudimentary bomb wired to the ignition. You wouldn't need much knowledge to make one. Just a Google search and you're there. Anyone inside wouldn't have stood a chance. Means and opportunity, going from the lax guards, established. Motive — killing Selby — unsure. Nothing from Forensics on the car. It was a ball of flame. What do you think? No fingerprints, DNA, none of the usual evidence.'

'Any luck from your side on Selby's computer?' I said, knowing the answer.

'Same answer. What do you think? Not a top priority for overtime on a weekend. They'll get stuck in tomorrow, but frankly I think you're in the driving seat.'

'Let's talk about Selby,' I said. 'I have two alternative theories, both centring around his role. The first is that he got cold feet on the money laundering and wanted out. The big boys snuffed him out in case he went to the police and told everything. The second is that he found out about the football scam and wanted a cut of the action as a price of turning a blind eye. Either way, he was desperate for money.'

'And which do you favour?' Palmer asked.

'The money laundering. That's a much bigger operation. Drugs money almost certainly: worth killing for. The football scam isn't a big enough operation to warrant planting a bomb. It may run into a million or so, but that will be small beer compared to the drugs money.'

'What's your time frame?' he said.

'We should be finished with football today, thanks to Anji and Valentine's hard work all weekend. We'll try to follow the money trail from the casinos and betting shops as the next stage. I've got an interim debrief at Zeus tomorrow afternoon, after a bit of fun to leaven the bread. I can be scant on the details, but I will have to come clean about the existence of the problems. I anticipate a full debrief on Friday and reports handed over at the meeting. How does that fit with you?'

'I'll hold off pulling in Simpson until Tuesday morning, if you give me everything you have on him, so that I can pass it all on to the Drugs Squad and the Serious Crimes guys as a watertight case. I'll keep you posted on what I can, if you do the same.'

'Sounds like a plan,' I said.
Who would have thought it?

* * *

'We had roast turkey for lunch,' said Cherry, at the start of my visit. 'You could cut the gravy into slices.'

She was sitting in an armchair next to her bed. I brought a hardback chair from the area at the end of the ward and sat opposite her holding her hand. 'We must have a celebration meal at Toddy's when we get you home.' Toddy's was a restaurant owned by Norman, where the chef was the ex-chief cook at Chelmsford in our time there. Toddy's mantra was get the best ingredients and treat them simply so that the flavours shone through. It was the in place to go in London and was booked up six weeks in advance. Norman always kept one large table unallocated till eight o'clock so that it could be free for us to show up if the mood caught us.

'I brought you some things,' I said.

'Not more grapes,' she said. 'Although if you did, I would thank you profusely and share them out with other patients as soon as you'd gone.'

'I liaised with Anji,' I said. 'So you have to thank her.' I started to unpack the bag I had brought. 'She said you would appreciate this lipstick — it's bright red and she said there's nothing like a lipstick in making a girl brighten up.'

'That's sweet.'

'Beryl made you a sandwich — smoked salmon on brown bread with a horseradish sauce. Enjoy.'

I picked out an ice pack and the small bottle of Chablis it was keeping cool. I poured some into the glass I had brought and handed it to her. She took a sip.

'Nectar,' she said. 'Well done you.'

'Morag went shopping and bought you these. Lacy nightdress and a Chinese silk wraparound. Let's show these other patients how a real girl dresses in hospital.'

'Black,' she said, 'my colour.'

'Any colour suits you,' I said.

'Flattery will get you everywhere.'

'I know a good joke about stamp collecting,' I said.

'I've heard it,' she said, 'and, believe me, it's not good.'

'Going stir crazy?' I said.

'I'm leading an escape committee digging a tunnel under the shower.'

'Just one more day,' I said, 'and we can all get back to normal, although I don't know what normal is for us.'

'How are the troops?' she asked. 'Tell me all the gossip, especially concerning Anji and Valentine. Are they engaged yet?'

'Good as,' I said. 'Anji is totally smitten. They're at the holding-hands stage, and Valentine stayed the night when they got back from dinner. I hope he reciprocates her feelings. I would hate to see her hurt.'

'He's a good lad,' Cherry said. 'He wouldn't deliberately hurt her. If it's not going to happen for them, he's nice enough to let her down gently. We should stand by, however, in case she takes it badly. You do the father figure and I'll do the big sister. Now tell me about this mysterious lunch date.'

'It was with the Lady Livia. Not a happy bunny. Apparently, no one likes me.'

'What else is new?' Cherry said.

'Ha ha. She has this master plan for the three daughters. They are to run all three divisions of Zeus. After that, there will only be Shapiro standing in their way. I don't know what they plan for him, but my guess is that it will be nasty.'

'Agree,' she said. 'What else?'

'Campion is dying, so she said. Lung cancer. She doesn't want me to spoil his last six months or so. Just an added reason why she wants us to get the hell out of there. I said no.'

'It's the honour thing again, isn't it? I bet she didn't understand.'

'Yes to both,' I said. 'We'll go ahead with tomorrow's plans and see what the reaction is from Campion and Shapiro.'

'And you think the stunt that you're going to pull is going to save us?'

'Can't do any harm,' I said. 'It will be fun, too. We haven't had much of that so far. If we fail, at least we'll exit on a high note.'

'I wish you good luck.'

We reverted from business to personal hats and talked about mundane things — it was the company that was important, not the topic of conversation. After half an hour or so, a bell rang and visitors began to get ready to leave.

'I'll pick you up tomorrow after my meeting with Campion and Shapiro. Be about five, I expect. Be great to have you home.'

'Be great to be back,' she said. A tear ran down her cheek.

I set off straight away. I didn't look back. I didn't want to see a flood of tears.

Since parking at the hospital — like all hospitals — was nigh impossible, I had parked at Tesco and walked the short distance — no more than fifteen minutes at a leisurely pace — to the Beamer.

Motorbikes. Was this going to be a day of motorbikes? There was a deep throat roar of a motorbike behind me. Far more power than what was needed in a supermarket car park. What is the point? I looked over my shoulder. There was the point. The motorbike had a passenger. The passenger had a gun. Hellfire!

Thud, thud, thud. I felt the bullets hit my left shoulder as I dived to the ground. I had escaped the first volleys by quick reactions, but I was now flat on the ground, making it easier for the gunman to pick his spot while I was lying flat. I tried to roll over and find a space under a parked car. The gap between car and car park was too small. I became resigned to my fate. My only hope was that the gunman was a lousy shot.

I heard a new roar. More tinny this time. Sounded familiar. The cavalry had arrived.

Arthur's van smashed into the motorbike and sent it spiralling head over heels in the air before falling to the ground.

The driver and the gunman lost their grip and the gun scattered over the ground. Arthur drove over the two bodies, pinning them down. They were our prisoners now.

'What should we do now?' he asked. 'Hospital or Palmer?'

There was a lot of blood coming from my shoulder. I felt no pain, the natural burst of adrenaline keeping it at bay, but I knew that wouldn't last long.

'As much as I like playing the hero,' I said. 'I think it should be ambulance first and police second. I can phone Palmer from the ambulance. These two guys aren't going anywhere. You stay here to sort out the police while I go in the ambulance.' I paused. 'Arthur, I've said it in the past and I'll say it again, you are a miracle. A lifesaver in my hour of need. The truest of friends.'

'Steady on,' he said. 'Anyway, that's what friends are for, isn't it? No more sentimental stuff. You'll have me welling up in a moment and tears don't suit me.'

'I think I need to sit down,' I said, suddenly feeling weak.

'You can sit in the van,' he said. 'A bit more weight won't make much of a difference to these guys. And, if it did, it would only be what they deserve.'

He supported me into the passenger seat of the van. I took out my phone.

'I'll do it,' he said. 'You should stay quiet. That shoulder shouldn't have too much movement. Is Palmer's number on your phone? Leave it all to me.'

I waited for him to finish the brief calls and took a deep breath. I winced. There was something about breathing that was not how it should be.

'All done,' he said. 'Won't be long.'

'How long have you been tailing me?' I asked.

'Since you left home,' he said. 'That's one of the advantages of having a white van. They're everywhere and all look alike. Plus no one wants to steal it. Ah, here comes your chariot, lights a'flashing, sirens set to burst our eardrums. See you later at the hospital. Don't go running any marathons till I get there. Good luck, Nick.'

* * *

'Not you again,' Palmer said, after straightening the blanket over my trolly in A&E. 'We have to stop meeting this way. My wife will start to get suspicious. OK, Shannon. Tell me all.'

I told him everything that had happened since leaving Cherry in the hospital to where I now lay.

'Someone doesn't like you,' he said.

'Only one?' I said. 'What news on the two underneath Arthur's van?'

'Contract muscle, we think. They've been hauled in a number of times — petty offences — and we've never been able to make anything stick. They won't get away with it this time. I'll give them a grilling, but they're not the kind to squeal. Plea bargain is a possibility, but I think they've gone too far for that to be feasible — you can't go into a supermarket car park and start shooting and expect to get away with it. What's the prognosis?'

'Three bullets in the left shoulder — as if that wasn't evident from the way I'm lying here. All passed through. Exit wounds show there's nothing to be dug out. I'm a lucky man, they say. They've just got to put in a few stitches, patch me up, pump me full of painkillers and then I can go home.'

'So,' Palmer said, 'are we back to the same people in your book as the bombing?'

'Definitely. We've found fraud, but nothing big enough to warrant this. Significant, but not to the degree to warrant a murder charge. Out of their league, whoever they may turn out to be. It's back to the only other possibility — money laundering. Any developments your end?'

'What do you think?'

'That you wouldn't be here if there were.'

'All in a day's work,' he said. 'How does the song go — a policeman's lot is not a happy one?'

'Not only a policeman's,' I said. 'Someone wants me off this case.'

'And what are you going to do?'

'Stick with it.'

'Just what I would have guessed,' he said. 'Stay lucky.'

CHAPTER SIXTEEN

It was Monday morning and the pain from the shoulder left me chewing on any painkillers I could lay my hands on, but it had to be carry on as usual. We had no commitments till the afternoon. We had a good start. Anji and Valentine made a discovery: something that might unlock the puzzle of Prometheus.

'It's a recently formed company,' said Anji, 'and because of that, the directors have not had to file any returns yet. They're still in the leeway period. It's an off-the-shelf company and that's all we know.'

'The good news,' Valentine said, 'is that because the company was formed in the last year, the scam they are pulling probably hadn't started back more than that. Helpful in our final bill with calculating the amount of the ten per cent clause?'

I nodded and looked at the import of his words. '*Our* final bill.'

'We've got an address for the registered office,' Anji said. 'I don't know whether it will help or not, but it might be worth a look.'

'No time like the present,' I said. 'You drive.'

'Vroom vroom!' she said.

'You drive carefully,' I said.

'Spoilsport.'

The address was in North London, not too far away. A rundown area with a high street with only about a seventy-five per cent occupancy rate, even with allowing for charity shops. There was the obligatory pawn shop. We parked up and had a look around. Why would someone give this as their address? It was a corner shop selling what they could from a limited range of goods, including some strange vegetables that would have had even Toddy perplexed. Anji got out of the Beamer and went for a closer look.

'Bingo,' Anji said when she came back. 'It's a postbox, an accommodation address. Very secretive. Spooksville USA.'

'Let's stay awhile and see if anything happens,' I said. 'While we're waiting, Valentine, tell us about your father. He keeps a low profile. Anything to hide?'

'Born in Portugal and came here when he was nine, not speaking any English. He was soon recognized as bright by his teachers. They pushed him on to the next step of learning by giving him special classes in English. He picked it up quickly and easily. The teachers realized he was destined for higher things and kept pushing him.

'When he came to Britain,' Valentine said, 'it was the era of grammar schools. He passed his 11+ and got a place at the local grammar school. Next, Cambridge to read English Language and Literature. Got a first.'

'Sounds like the American Dream comes to Britain,' I said. 'Then what?'

'Became a journalist. Stints in the papers and TV. He did some foreign correspondent work for ITV. After a while, he said he didn't want to live that life for ever, that he wanted to spend more time with his family, put roots down. A job in the Publishing Division here came up and he showed a talent for management as well as a flair for what news to feature. His future was now mapped out.'

I was listening to Valentine while watching the door to the shop. The vegetables proved popular.

'What about Shapiro the man?' I said. 'What makes him tick?

'He's a socialist and fights for justice for the man on the street. He dislikes people who ride roughshod over others. He described himself one time as someone who wanted to be a beacon of light in the face of so much that was wrong in the country. He's a moral person and tries to uphold old-fashioned standards. Oh, he's a vegan — was one before it became a cause in its own right — old values, again.'

'Does he have a sense of humour?' I asked. 'How is he going to react to what we are planning?

'I think he will see the point of what we're trying to do. Can't guarantee it, but I think he'll be positive.'

A motorbike rider came up and went into the shop. Emerged a moment later clutching some letters. He stuffed them in his saddle bag and headed off.

'Follow him,' I said to Anji. 'See where he goes.'

Anji waited a moment so that she wouldn't be obviously following him and pulled out after him. He rode on for ten minutes or so, during which time it was increasingly difficult to follow him as he dodged in and out of the traffic and made a drop off. He then set out again. He made another drop off and I gave up. It was impossible to follow him.'

'Anyone ride a motorbike?' I asked.

'Not me,' said Valentine. 'It would scare me rigid.'

'I do,' said Anji. 'My granddad taught me. He was a motorbike nut. I know some tricks. Got a licence and everything — a full set of leathers I've been dying to wear for ages.'

Let's not go there. I didn't think Valentine's blood pressure could take it.

Anji had come up trumps again. How lucky we were to have her.

'I have a plan,' I said. No one groaned yet. 'It involves a tennis player scratching her naked bottom.' Now they groaned. 'Trust me. We're going to have some fun. Anji, phone the office and ask Morag or Beryl to get these things. Tally ho.'

Anji and Valentine giggled.

* * *

The taxi dropped Anji, Valentine and me in the car park at Leytonstone High Street at three o'clock. I was already hot in the London Fog overcoat I was wearing. I kept my left hand in the pocket Beryl had worked on and told myself it wouldn't be long before I could take it off.

Arthur was there waiting for us. A motley collection of what could only be described as bouncers stood in a group smoking. Valentine approached them and opened the briefcase he was guarding. Inside were ten lots of two hundred pounds, already counted out, and ten lots of two thousand pounds per person separated by paper clips. Arthur and Valentine worked their way round the group and began to dole out the money. I reminded myself to trust Arthur in his recruitment decisions and that no one would go AWOL with the money. They would not want to raise Arthur's wrath.

'All set?' I said to Arthur.

'Relax,' he said. 'They all know what to do. I've been over it three times.'

'They're clear that it is the three-thirty race at Plumpton?'

Arthur nodded wearily.

'And that the bet is each way on Golden Boy.'

There are two kinds of bet. To win — you only make a profit if your horse wins the race — and each way, where half of your bet is on the horse to win and the other half on your horse being in the top three, being "placed", although there are certain rules, depending on the number of horses in the race. For each way, you get a third of the odds if your horse is placed.

'No sweat,' said Arthur.

'OK,' I said. 'Let's put this show on the road.'

Anji, Valentine and I walked to the betting shop, took a deep breath and went inside. There were about half a dozen people inside going through the form guide, looking at the monitors or playing the slots and I hoped none of them got in our way. Over to Valentine now.

He knocked on the thick glass door to the cashiers and prepared to go through the script. The woman in charge, in what was her uniform of black suit, white blouse and heels, recognized him and tapped in the entry code. We filed through.

'Us again,' he said. 'We need to have a second look at procedures. Check out a few things, test the system.'

'I thought you were done here,' the manageress said. 'You seemed pleased with what you saw last time.'

'Indeed,' Valentine said. 'We were so impressed that we want to see what other branches can learn if they followed your lead. A lot of team points for you. Maybe even some kind of bonus. Who knows?'

I was impressed. He was a good liar, a useful trait in our business. Stage one complete. We were in. I moved to the back of the office and Anji and Valentine moved in front of me, hiding me from the view of the manager. Stage two ticked.

I checked my watch — like casinos, there are no clocks inside betting shops, so that the customers lose track of time and how long they have been there. Three-fifteen. The shop started to fill up as Arthur and our Baker Street Irregulars arrived and began to fill in their betting slips.

According to the monitors, the odds for Golden Boy were six to one. Those were the odds that we would take instead of the odds at the start of the race. About the only guarantee we would get from now on. Time for the third and final phase.

I unbuttoned my coat and slipped my right hand inside. Transferred the contents from my left hand to right. I took the long bolt cutters and placed them over the cable that controlled the link to the Zeus system. I gripped the insulated handles and crossed my fingers that I wouldn't get electrocuted. Caught Arthur's eye and sliced the cable in two.

The monitors flickered for a moment but, being on a different circuit, held firm. The pictures showed the horses in the parade ring.

'Move to paper,' shouted the manageress.

Two queues formed in front of the cashiers and the men started to hand over their betting slips and the two thousand in cash. It was three twenty-seven when everyone had finished.

The monitor showed the race without sound. If you didn't recognize the jockeys' colours it was hard to tell which horse was which. Golden Boy was number five and that helped when the saddle numbers were not obscured by other horses or if the jockeys' silks were indistinguishable.

Golden Boy took an early lead — not usually a good sign since, if going too fast, the horse would be tired and move back in the field towards the end. It was an eight-furlong race — one mile in real money — and sure enough, the horse had over-extended itself and other horses came through to challenge. It struggled for a heart-stopping minute but held on to come third. Payout time. The queues started again. Arthur stood by the door with the briefcase and took the money from his friends as they exited the shop.

Valentine phoned for a taxi and we prepared to leave. A man in an orange jacket came in. I beckoned him over and got the manageress to buzz him through. He had come, as arranged, to wire in a new link to Zeus. Ever thoughtful Shannon: I didn't want to see the manageress get into trouble. It wasn't her fault, and it would be a lesson for the whole of the region. It was also fun.

* * *

We were on time for our interim debrief with Sir Gerald and Shapiro. They had smiles on their faces. Good to be popular again. Valentine put the briefcase on the table in front of me, the money inside sorted into three piles.

'This an interim debrief,' I said. 'I'll give you a full presentation on Friday, but there are some things you will want to address before then. Security — the guards and so on — is one of those issues. Less than an hour ago we broke the system of your betting shop in Leytonstone.' I took out the three piles of money. I placed the smallest pile on the table in front of them. 'This is what it cost us to set up the scam.' Time for the second pile, bigger this time. 'This is what we staked.' Lastly time for the third pile. 'And this is what we scammed from you. Around twenty thousand pounds. We could have gone for more, but this was just a demonstration.'

'How did you manage it?' said Shapiro.

'It was simple. We just gained access to the office and cashiers' desks and I cut the wire to the Zeus system. As we placed our ten bets of twenty-thousand pounds there was no feedback from the computer, so there was no effect on the odds.'

I pushed the pile of winnings in front of Sir Gerald. He pushed it back. 'Keep it, Shannon my boy,' he said. 'Cost of an expensive lesson. We need to tighten the security of our branches. What next?'

'You could beef up the security of your systems here. In light of the bomb, you should have photo ID and arrangements for entry of non-staff to be handled at the barrier — cards should be authorized and handed out from there. No unauthorized entry permitted.'

Campion turned to Shapiro. 'Why don't we have photo ID?' he said.

'If you remember, Gerald, we got one of those booths where you can take passport photos. It arrived on the day of our Christmas party. We got through a month's supply in one night. Memories for everyone.'

'Get another one and put it in a locked room,' Campion said.

'Fair point,' said Shapiro. 'Nothing like the bomb in Selby's car can happen again. Next?'

'You have to take a look at your procedures regarding money laundering. We're still investigating, but I am certain that the casinos and betting shops around London are being used for those purposes. At the moment, there are no limits on cash betting. We'll give you full details on Friday, but you should be making a plan of new regulations you will propose.'

I took a breath and looked round to Anji and Valentine. They seemed calm and confident enough to be in front of some of the captains of industry without being overawed. Especially for Valentine, as his father might be judging him.

I continued. 'There is a scam going on around the setting of odds. The interface between odds setter and watcher needs to be less cosy, shall we say. This fraud could run into millions. As I said, I'll tell you more on Friday, but at least two people will have to be sacked. I'm obliged to inform the Fraud Squad of our findings, but it be a while before they catch up with us. You need to get whoever does your press office to start working on some releases.

'Finally,' I said, 'we have ourselves a tricky situation. Your replacement of Selby, Violet, is banning me from any future interviews with her staff and access to her systems. Effectively, I'm off the case. I need some authorization from you if I am to carry on. Basically, countermanding her orders.'

'As you say,' said Sir Gerald, 'tricky. What you are doing is too valuable to be stopped. I'll have a word with her. Tell her that power carries its own responsibilities. Carry on doing what you're doing. I think I talk from both of us here in saying we are impressed by what you are doing. We made the right choice in hiring you, even if you do make us look stupid at times. Roll on Friday.'

Indeed.

* * *

We met up with Arthur where he was waiting in the reception area. I passed him the briefcase. 'Guard that till you can get it into the new safe. Take two grand out and pay your friends a bonus of another two hundred. They did well. You did well.'

Arthur went off to his van and we waited for our cab to arrive. It was only a couple of minutes and didn't harm our feeling of elation of a successful meeting. It was indeed fun and we were back on the case. I wondered what sort of a tongue-wagging he would get from the Lady Livia. Poor guy, but there are times when you have to do the right thing and not take the easy route.

'Now I'm off to pick up Cherry,' I said when we were back at Zeus. 'Get her home to where she belongs and celebrate her return.'

I climbed painfully into the Beamer and drove to the hospital. My heart was thudding from my excitement at the prospect of seeing her out of the hospital bed and sitting next to me as we drove back. I was buzzed into the ward and went to Cherry's bed. There was another woman in it.

'I'm looking for Cherry Walker,' I said at the nursing station. 'You've moved her.'

'She went home about an hour ago,' a nurse said. 'A man came and said he was a driver for a Mr Campion. She was so keen to go that she jumped at the chance of a lift home there and then. She said you would understand.'

I told myself it made perfect sense with Cherry having gone stir crazy. I drove home a little faster than normal and parked up. Once inside the building. I checked my office and the river room. She wasn't there.

Morag walked over to me. 'Where's Cherry?' she said.

'I thought she was with you,' I said. 'The hospital said she was being taken home by a driver sent by Campion. That was over an hour ago. She should be home by now. Is there any chance she went upstairs without you seeing her? Maybe she went up to change?'

'I can't see how,' Morag said. 'I've been here all afternoon.'

'I'll go and check,' I said.

I went upstairs to the top floor and looked around our apartment. She wasn't there. Then the realization hit me.

Cherry had disappeared.

CHAPTER SEVENTEEN

I called Palmer to see if there was anything he could do. He came twenty minutes later. We went into the river room and he watched me pacing up and down. It was either that or sitting down and putting my head in my hands and that wouldn't do any good.

'So you're sure Campion doesn't know anything about this,' Palmer said. 'Maybe he did send a car and they broke down. These things do happen.'

'I've checked with him. He didn't send a car.'

'Then you'll get a call soon. There will be demands. Either you obey or they will do something to Cherry. Doesn't bear thinking about.'

'Did you get anywhere in finding Simpson's address?'

'Stalled so far, but no one wants to do anything to give a clue to the money launderers and drugs baron that we're on their trail. They want the headman, full stop. They're going to hang fire and wait for a break. I tried to persuade them to do something, but they outrank me. Outrank my boss, too.'

'How can that be so?' I said. 'We're talking about a woman's life here.'

'Oh, they'll act eventually. They'll be working behind the scenes now, trying to see if they can get a breakthrough.

Whether they'll get anywhere quick enough I don't know. All I can say is that I'll do everything I can to get Cherry back.'

The phone rang and I snatched it up. I put the call on speaker so that Palmer could hear.

'Shannon?' a man said. The voice had been altered by some piece of computerized software that made it sound like he was gargling with a harmonica.

'Speaking,' I said. 'Say your piece. What is it that you want me to do?'

'That's what I like to hear, Shannon. A man open to discuss a deal. If you want to see Walker again, and in one piece, listen well to what I have to say. Ready?'

'Don't drag this out,' I said.

'Don't deny me my fun. I often think there's not enough fun in the world. The world would be a better place for a bit more fun, don't you think?'

'Speak or I'll end this call and you won't get what you want. I'm hanging up in one minute. No more playing around with me.'

'I reckon you're bluffing, but, anyway, this is what you have to do. Listen carefully. You will delete all material on your computer relating to Zeus. You will shred all relevant papers. You will forget everything you've done in the last two weeks. Lastly, you will not go to the police. I will send my computer whizz-kid to check that you have complied with my demands. He will come at midnight. When he's happy, I'll release Cherry. How is that sounding?'

'I want to speak to Cherry. I'll do nothing till I know she's safe. Take it or leave it.'

'You'd make a good poker player. Again, I think you're bluffing, but I'll indulge you. Wait.'

There was a silence that seemed to last forever.

'Stick to the script,' the man said. 'Go ahead.'

'Shannon,' Cherry said, 'I am not harmed. I am tied up hand and foot, so there is no chance of me being able to escape. I have been threatened with torture if you don't do as he says. It will be a slow and painful death. You're a gambler, Shannon. Play the odds.'

There was the sound of the phone landing on the floor.

'I told you to stick to the script,' we heard the man say. 'One last time, Shannon. Do what I say or I'll start to chop her fingers off and send them in pieces to you. I have nothing to lose. I'm already facing a murder charge for killing Selby, so one more won't make any difference. Midnight, Shannon.'

The phone went dead.

'At least we know she's alive and unharmed,' Palmer said. 'That's good news.'

'As you say, good news, but I'm puzzled. The man said to stick to the script, but his reaction meant she had added something. "Gambler. Play the odds". What is she trying to tell me?'

'Are you going to comply?' Palmer asked.

'I don't seem to have any option,' I said, 'but I have till midnight and I'm going to use every minute of that time to work out a way of getting Cherry back.'

'Do you trust him to keep his word?'

'If he reneges on the deal, we're in no different a situation than we are now. It seems to be the only chance.'

I came out of the river room and found Morag still working. I asked her to gather everybody. I needed total commitment on any future action. It might be useful, too, to have some fresh input.

Everyone started to come into the room. There wasn't a face that wasn't glum. Worry lines showed at maximum capacity. Morag brought me a glass of water and the painkillers I had left handy on her desk. I swallowed twice the dose. What the hell did I care at this moment in time?

'The situation is this,' I said. 'Cherry has been abducted. The man who had kidnapped her has issued some demands. Basically, all the work on Zeus has to be destroyed. Someone will come at midnight to check I have obeyed instructions.

Obviously, the police must not be involved. DI Palmer here will need to go. We can't run the risk that someone reports him present.'

'I understand,' he said. 'Just to make it clear, I will be ready for any help you need, even if it means I'm working in a private capacity.'

'I don't like leaving a job undone, as you all know,' I said, 'but I'm not giving up without a fight. I spoke to Cherry on the phone and she's unhurt. She said something puzzling. I think it was supposed to be a clue. She said something about being a gambler and playing the odds. If any of you think you might have an inkling of what she was trying to say, I'll be eternally grateful.'

Silence while they cogitated.

'The kidnapper hasn't said anything about the other side of the Zeus job, so I want to act as normal. Morag, did you manage to arrange the motorbike?'

She nodded.

'Beryl, did you get the posters?'

Another nod.

'Then, Anji, you need to stick with the plan. Head off in the morning and do your bit.'

'Will do,' she said. 'I think I'll be better off being occupied in any case.'

'Valentine, stand by in case Anji needs any help.'

'Be my pleasure,' he said. 'Any help I can give, I'm there for you.'

'I know we had a vote on what we should do, but if any of you want to bow out, I will completely understand.'

No one, as I hoped, as I expected, said anything.

'I'll go,' said Palmer. 'I don't want to seem to be involved. Best to be careful. I'm there if you need me. Good luck, Shannon.'

Then gloom manifested itself again. No one had anything to say. Then Valentine popped up.

'This may be nothing,' he said. 'Probably a waste of our time really.'

'Spit it out, Valentine. All contributions welcome.'

He took a deep breath.

'It's just the time we played the odds was with Cherry at the casino. What if she is trying to get you to go to the casino?'

'And find Simpson!' I shouted. 'We've got to find Simpson, that was what she was saying. Find Simpson and then go upstream to the top man! Valentine, you're a genius. Thank you from the bottom of my heart.'

Valentine blushed.

'Arthur, get yourself ready. We're going to Lakeside, and not for the shopping.'

'That's good,' he said. 'I hate shopping.'

No one said anything, preferring to be silent about his ever-present donkey jacket.

'How's the shoulder?' he said.

'Good enough to drive,' I said. 'That's all that's important right now. I imagine, unless we're very lucky, that we're going to be doing a lot of driving tonight.'

'Anything I can do?' said Morag. 'Make you a sandwich and fish out the Kendal mint cake and a blanket?'

'You missed out the bit about the spade,' I said. 'I think a sandwich and a couple of water bottles would probably be good. We're going to be sitting around waiting for the right moment to come up.'

'White bread for me,' Arthur said. 'I've tried the brown bread and the one with seeds on and I reckon they're overrated. Give me good old-fashioned white bread anytime. Got any smoked salmon? I like the one that comes with the mustard and dill sauce. Horseradish will do instead. I don't want to be picky.'

'I'll do what I can,' said Morag, before Arthur went on about his love of jammy dodgers.

'This not a picnic,' I said. 'We're going to need to be hard men, not going to Glyndebourne.'

'Only trying to be helpful,' Morag said. 'To do something while the night drags on.'

'In that case, I'll have the same as Arthur. Thanks, Morag. No offence.'

'None taken,' she said. 'It's a strange time. We all have to do what we can.'

'Indeed,' I said. 'I've just enough time to change into more hard-men clothes and then we'll be off. I'd sooner be miles early than miss out. That's not an option. Let's go.'

I put on a pair of black chinos, a black T-shirt and a black leather jacket. Be hard to spot me in the dark. That could be crucial. I sprayed some fragrance on my neck in case things got close up. Naw, only joking. Got to keep your sense of humour in this dark time, keep your other feelings under control. You might need to you use them later.

Off we went.

* * *

'Are you going to eat your sandwich?' Arthur said, as we were speeding down the M25.

'No,' I said.

'Me, too,' he said.

'I only did it to make Morag feel useful,' I said.

'Me, too,' he said.

'How's the shoulder?' he said.

'Hurts like hell,' I said.

'If you want me to drive,' he said, 'we can pull over to the hard shoulder and I'll take over.'

'Thanks for the offer, Arthur, but I need something to concentrate on that isn't about Cherry and what they might be doing to her.'

'Understood,' he said. 'How far are we going to go with Simpson?'

'As far as it takes. No prisoners.'

CHAPTER EIGHTEEN

We parked up as close as we could get to the casino. Sat there looking at our watches. As the time grew nearer, we stepped out of the car and stood a little way back from the entrance and out of sight of the bouncers so that we were ready to pounce. Waiting is the hardest part.

Simpson came out of the casino at his usual time. He was a creature of habit and that predictability made him vulnerable. It was our only advantage. I told him how great it was to see him again. I dug a ballpoint pen in his back.

'This is a Browning Hi-Power 9mm handgun. You do just as I say,' I said, 'or I'm going to blow your spine to smithereens. You might survive, although personally I doubt it, but you'll never walk again. Now tell your driver you've met a friend and you'll be having dinner with him and then he will be taking you home. Tell him he won't be needed tonight.'

He did what I said. It's hard not to when you have a gun in your back. Disobedience is not an option.

'Who are you?' he said. 'Why are you doing this? If it's money, I don't have any cash. All my money goes straight to the bank.'

'We can go into all that later,' I said. 'Say hello to my friend and get into the car.'

Arthur wrapped an arm around Simpson, led him to the Beamer, manhandled him into the back and then climbed in after him. All very cosy. I put the pen back in my pocket. Mightier than the sword.

'We're going to get you home and have a little chat,' I said. 'I've already set the sat nav.'

'How do you know where I live?'

'Before we make any move, we do our homework. A little bird in the cashiers' department told us. Part of the information you filled in when initially sorting out your bank account.'

'Then you should know that you're out of your league,' he said. 'The people I work for will smash you to pieces.'

'They will have to catch us first. Alright in the back there, Arthur?'

'Snug as a bug in a rug,' he said. 'Aren't we, Mr Simpson? I said, "aren't we, Mr Simpson?" Answer or I'll break a finger.'

'Yes, yes,' Simpson said, his voice faltering. 'Like your goon said, snug.'

'Did he just racially slur me? Did he call me a coon?'

'No. He just called you a goon.'

'Well, that's alright then,' Arthur said.

It took us thirty minutes to get to his house. In companiable silence? I don't think so.

It was an Edwardian town house in Greenwich, almost home territory, delightfully restored to its former glory with everything in keeping. No double-glazing here — good old-fashioned sash windows. Arthur got out of the car and walked round to the rear door and hauled Simpson out by the scruff of his neck.

'Key, my friend,' I said. No harm in being polite. 'Unlock or we smash the door down.'

Simpson's hands were shaking as he tried to fit the key in the lock. I took it from him and unlocked the door. There was a long hallway with doors leading off it and a staircase to the two floors above. I looked inside each door until I found the kitchen — nice oak worktops and matching cupboards.

All very twee. We went inside and Arthur threw Simpson on the floor.

'Now for that little chat,' I said. 'Your friends have a partner of mine. All I need from you is an address. Give.'

'If you think I'm going to tell you that, then you must be mad. I'd be a dead man walking if I talk.'

'Stamp on his left hand,' I said to Arthur.

There was a sickening crunch of bones.

'Sorry about that, Nick,' Arthur said. 'I didn't mean to do it that hard,'

'No problem, Arthur. Do exactly the same on his right hand.'

'No!' Simpson shouted. 'If I talk, I'll get a bullet between my eyes.'

'No loss to society there, then,' I said.

Simpson's right hand was cradling his shattered left. Arthur used his heavy-duty boot with the steel toecaps to manoeuvre the two hands apart and get the right hand flat on the floor. He stamped. The sound of the bones breaking repeated itself.

Still Simpson wouldn't talk.

'Let's take a trip upstairs,' I said. 'Arthur, help him up there. You know what to do if he resists.'

'Break his third hand?' Arthur said.

The small bedroom at the back suited my purpose. We put Simpson on the single bed temporarily.

'I reckon we need some fresh air,' I said.

I moved over to the sash window and opened it up as far as it would go. About right, I thought.

Arthur and I picked him off the bed and carried him horizontally to the window. Lifted him outside until only his feet were inside.

'If you scream, we're going to drop you. If you don't give us what we want, we're going to drop you. Aren't many options.'

His whole body started to shake. If he was trying to break our grip; that wasn't going to be doing him any good.

Must have been a drop of about forty feet. He probably wouldn't survive. We made a movement where it felt like we had lost our grip. He started to cry.

'Let me in,' he shouted. 'I'll tell you what you want. Please let me in.'

We hauled him in and laid him on the bed.

'Fire away,' I said.

He gave us an address in the seaside town of Frinton, Essex, home to the wealthy retired. Just about into the twenty-first century, but would rather not have been. The Beamer would gobble that up in less than an hour. The question of the moment was what to do with Simpson.

'Let's get him downstairs,' I said to Arthur.

Not as easy as it would seem. He needed lifting because, with broken hands, he couldn't grip the bannisters. Arthur, basically, had to lift him down each step.

'What do you reckon?' Arthur said. 'Clothesline or gaffer tape, neither of which we have at the moment.'

'Improvise,' I said.

Arthur looked round the kitchen. There was a TV on one of the worktops. He yanked out the long aerial cable. He looked again. Electric kettle. Cable off that, too. He brought both cables to the floor where Simpson was laying and tied his hands and feet together. There were plenty of things we could use as a gag. Arthur chose a big wad of kitchen roll.

'Before we leave you,' I said, 'where's your mobile phone?'

'Pocket,' he groaned.

I dug in his pocket and took out his mobile phone and placed it on the floor by Arthur. 'You know what to do,' I said.

Arthur's boot stamped down, reducing the phone to the state of completely smashed.

I did a recce around the house and found a telephone on each floor. I pulled them out of the sockets — no landline calls anymore to add to no mobile.

'I tell you what we're going to do,' I said. 'In a moment we're going to leave you. When we have Cherry back, we'll

156

call an ambulance. You're just going to have to wait a while. Spend the time wisely. Think about all the bad things you have done and how you can absolve them.' I stuffed the kitchen roll inside his mouth. 'Till then, my friend, thank us for not killing you.'

* * *

The house at Frinton was a large, thatched cottage with a biscuit-tin lid of open countryside. No neighbours as far as the eye could see. It was L-shaped and had dormer windows on the second storey. Would be a shame to get blood on such an idyllic picture, but needs must.

There seemed little sense in ringing the bell. There was CCTV, and whoever was inside wouldn't have let us in anyway. Arthur stood back and kicked the door in. Sometimes the simple things work best.

We burst inside to see a man running up the stairs. We ran after him. He went into a room and did the pointless act of slamming the door shut and locking it. If Arthur had the strength to kick down the front door, then this flimsy bedroom door wouldn't stand a chance. I stood back to give Arthur some room and watched as his foot connected to the door and it became splinters.

Cherry was tied to a chair. The man stood over her with a gun.

'If you come any closer, I'll shoot,' he said.

Mexican standoff. We stayed where we were, with an intention of edging closer if given a chance.

'Glad to see you still alive, Walker,' I said.

'Just glad?' she said.

'Well you know how I hate to show emotion.'

The man studied us. He was tall and thin — high-adrenaline lifestyle, I guessed — with startling green eyes that hinted at envy.

'What are we going to do now?' he said.

I felt like saying something cheesy, like *the game is up.*

'The game is up,' I said, unable to resist. It might make him turn his attention away from Cherry. That meant he might block out both her and Arthur. Might even make him smile. Easier to do a deal with.

'I heard you were a joker. Shannon, I presume.'

'And you are?' I said.

'The name's not material,' he said. 'What is relevant is that I'm the person with the gun. That means I control the situation. So, I'll tell you what to do.'

'That is a theoretical advantage,' I said. 'What do you think, Arthur?'

'Theoretical,' he said. 'Definitely theoretical.'

'Can we do without the comedy duo?' the man said. 'This is serious. I will blow her brains out if you don't do as I say.'

'Which is?' I said.

I had a feeling that he hadn't thought this through.

There was a long pause.

'Don't move,' he said.

'We've done that bit,' I said. 'What comes next?'

'Lay down your weapons.'

'We don't have any weapons,' I said, 'other than a Swiss army penknife, if that counts.'

'Hurry up,' Arthur said. 'This is getting tedious.'

'In the extreme,' I added.

'Sod this!' I heard Arthur say behind me before launching himself at the man. He caught him with a horizontal double kick at the man's chest who fell heavily on to the floor. Arthur kicked the gun away and planted his right boot on the man's chest.

'How did you know he wouldn't shoot?' I said to Arthur.

'What did I always say?' he said. 'Watch the eyes. The eyes will always tell you what your opponent will do next. Plus the fact, of course, that if you see a six-foot five thug coming toward you, who are you going to shoot? Not the woman, for sure.'

I untied Cherry and gave her a big hug. 'Good to see you again, Walker.'

'You must have worked fast, Shannon,' she said. 'Thanks. Especially to you, Arthur.'

She stood on tiptoe to plant a kiss on his cheek.

'Once you've got it, you don't lose it,' he said.

'Time to call Palmer,' I said.

I rang him and explained the situation. He said he would make the necessary calls — and there were lots of them — and be here in an hour.

'How did you get here so quickly?' Cherry asked.

'We dropped in on Simpson — the guy from the casino like the clue you gave me — and had a chat. We tried to reason with him, to no avail. During this time, he unluckily suffered some problems with his hands.'

'We broke them,' Arthur said. 'Still wouldn't talk.'

'Don't tell me,' said Cherry. 'You didn't pull the window trick, did you?'

'Never fails,' said Arthur, his foot still planted on the man's chest. 'If it works for Lee Marvin, it'll work for me. *Point Blank*, it was called. Follow in the footsteps of giants. Nothing wrong with that.'

* * *

The local police arrived first. I wondered what they were thinking when they found the front door lying on the floor. Red alert, I thought. I asked Cherry to go downstairs and tell them that the situation was under control.

Two police officers — one male, one female — followed her up the stairs and into the small bedroom. It started to feel crowded. We pointed to the gun on the floor and the male police officer picked it up gingerly with a pen and bagged it. The second officer handcuffed the man — still nameless — and manhandled him down the stairs. We told the police officers the story so far and were told to make a full statement in person the next day. I guessed it was way out of their comfort zone.

Palmer arrived, and I felt he might return things to as normal as was possible. I told him first about Simpson and how an ambulance would be needed as well as the police. There must be a stash of cash there.

'You're beginning to be predictable,' Palmer said. 'One dead or approaching it on every case. I think I won't go in the office anymore. I should just follow you around with a SOCO team on my heels. So, Simpson fell down the stairs, did he?'

'He needs to be more careful,' said Arthur. 'Going too fast and lost a step. He needs to take it more carefully.'

'Anyway,' I said, 'he's there for the picking. The game is over for him. Offer him witness protection and he'll — what do you say? — cough.'

'We usually say sing,' he said.

'I'll remember that for next time,' I said.

'Please don't go down that route,' Palmer said. 'I'm not sure my blood pressure can take all this excitement.'

Cherry told him the events from her side and how she had been rescued by the dynamic duo. Palmer tried to be unimpressed, but failed. He looked at me.

'So that's what happened,' he said.

'Gospel,' I said. 'Some of it even true.'

'Right,' he said. 'We best let you get home and have you make statements there.'

'While they're at it,' I said, 'there's a computer man coming at midnight. Might help the case. Be good to arrest him.'

'I'll handle the call now,' he said. 'It won't be long till officers arrive here en masse. They'll be the Drugs Squad, the Fraud Squad and officers of the Serious Crimes Unit. The less you say to them, the better. We've got this man — whatever his name turns out to be — for possession of an offensive weapon and Simpson for money laundering. It will be hard for even a hotshot lawyer to get them off. Simpson will squeal, I reckon, and then the whole house of cards will fall down.'

* * *

I gave Cherry my phone as I pulled away from the house so that she could call home and let them know she was safe. She was also able to tell them not to delete anything on the computer and that a local bobby would handle the situation with the computer man.

There was little traffic on the roads at that time of night and we were home in thirty minutes. The reception that Cherry got was amazing. Hugs and kisses all round. Morag made her some coffee and gave her a small glass of brandy.

'I bet you thought that life away from the Fraud Squad was going to be a doddle,' I said to Cherry. 'That the biggest drawback was that it wasn't challenging enough. That it was going to be dull.'

'Nothing's ever dull when you're around,' she said.

'Right, my darling,' I said to Cherry. 'Time for all of us to get some sleep, if that is possible with all the adrenaline surging through our bodies. Tomorrow is a new day. Lots to do. Good night and thanks to all of you. We're on the home stretch now. By Friday, it will all be over and back to normal. If we can remember normal, that is.'

CHAPTER NINETEEN

The sight of Anji in motorbike leathers was something to behold. Skintight with long flowing blonde hair. Valentine took a selfie of her and himself while the rest of us stood agog. The rest of us minus Cherry, that is. I had left her finally sleeping: she, and therefore I, had spent a disturbed night. She had tossed and turned in between small naps — at one point getting up and making herself a cup of tea and just staring out of the window at the river. During the short naps she had mumbled and her legs and arms had done a dance, at some times digging me in the ribs or kicking me in the shins. I told myself that things would pass and she would be the old Cherry again soon. The Cherry that I loved.

It was Tuesday morning; we had three full days to pull everything together before the final debrief. OK, if necessary, we could ask for more time, but we had made a commitment and I didn't like not delivering on a deal. Anji and Valentine were now ready to pull the poster trick. Valentine would set off to deliver the poster in its long cardboard tube, Anji ready to follow him and wait for the delivery bike to call. If he called. That was the weakness in the plan, but sometimes, like the night before, you have to hope Lady Luck is on your side.

The rest of the week was going to be all about detail. There were loose ends to tie up, and everything had to be covered and ready to be subjected to examination with a fine-tooth comb. It was all about establishing proof. Evidence.

Norman and I were in my office talking about the structure of the report.

'Can you give me some anecdotes about cash?' I asked him.

'More than you ever wish to know,' he replied. 'Do you want them in alphabetical order or by size of fraud?'

'Can you do outrageous?' I asked.

'You've come to the right man,' he said.

Cherry walked in. She was wearing skinny jeans and a white vest that showed off her coffee-cream skin. What little make-up she used had been immaculately applied. She had showered and I could smell the apricot aroma of the shampoo she used. She stood beside me and put a hand on my shoulder.

'How are you this morning?' Norman asked. 'Better, I hope.'

'Almost there,' she said. 'Approaching normal, but not quite there yet.' She shivered. 'He was going to cut my finger off and send it to you to make you do whatever he said. He would have done it, too. Kept smiling while he felt the finger and practised with the knife.'

'All over now,' I said. 'He didn't beat us. He didn't beat us because we are a unit that sticks together and stays together, whatever we have to face. That makes us strong. You know, Cherry, we knew the risks and what we might be facing, but no one dissented.'

'For which I'm grateful. Eternally grateful.' She shook her head as if trying to clear it. 'Right. Enough of that. What can I do?'

'Boring old reporting,' I said. 'I think it's best if you take the section on the football scam and I take the one on money laundering. No memories for you until it's absolutely necessary. Anji is out on the cardboard-tube trick, but Valentine will be back soon. I've got Norman here coming up with some examples on the lure of cash as context. It's a case of nose to the grindstone, which is what none of us likes. Soon be over, though.'

Morag came into the room. 'Inspector Palmer is here,' she said. 'Shall I let him in or is it too soon?'

Best for Cherry to get any memories of Monday out of the way, I thought, to move away from the past. Clear the mind, hopefully.

'Show him in,' I said. 'Maybe we could all have a coffee, if you don't mind.'

'Coming up,' she said.

Palmer came in and we all moved to the conference table. He offered Cherry his hand and then withdrew it. He hugged her instead. 'I so hope you're doing well. Must have been harrowing for you. Try to block it out of your memory, saving that for nicer things. It will take a while, but it will fade, believe me.'

'Come and take a seat, inspector. Coffee's on its way. Plus drip mats.'

'And how are you doing, Shannon, after your night-time adventures? Shame about Simpson falling done the stairs, but these things happen. A lot of draughts coming through that window, too. The room was getting chilly. I shut it. Just before any of my various compatriots arrived. Didn't want them getting a chill.'

'How thoughtful,' I said. 'Any progress to report? Anything to cheer us up?'

'Lots,' he said. 'Simpson is singing like a bird. That's his future sorted — might get away with five years if he's got a sympathetic judge, which is unlikely. Our mystery man, who is the boss of the drug business, is reluctant at the moment, but we've got possession of the gun to keep him in custody while we join the dots. We'll oppose bail. I don't think even with a hotshot lawyer — which he is bound to have — he'll get away without a ten-year stretch. The gun makes bail a lost cause for him.'

Morag brought the coffee in with a tray with sugar and a couple of spoons. I watched Palmer put in three heaped spoonfuls — even too much for me, and I have a sweet tooth. He hesitated as to where he would place his spoon and finished up putting it on the tray without a little paper napkin for such a purpose.

'We should all be thankful for Arthur saving the day,' I said. 'For someone who takes time for his brain to process things, he did extremely well. Do we have a name for the man with the gun?'

'If he's to be believed, it's Merriweather, which is kind of ironic. He won't be seeing any weather for a long time, merry or otherwise.' He permitted himself a little smile. 'And what's happening chez Shannon?'

'We have a fraud which I think we'll not pass on to the Fraud Squad. We'll use it as a bargaining chip to help clean the Augean stables.'

'Hercules?' he said. 'Surely you can come up with something more obscure than that.'

'I could, but then I remembered I was talking to a police officer.'

'Hah, hah,' he said. 'That segues nicely into another bit of news. I'm not retiring for a while. I'm being promoted to Chief Inspector, something I think I should be thanking you for, because of your input. The wife isn't too happy, but sees the bright side of me not getting under her feet all the time.'

'Well, congratulations,' we said in unison.

'You deserve it for trusting us.' I said. 'Not many police officers would have had the courage to do that.'

'There's some unhappy bunnies, though. We closed down a money laundering machine and arrested a drugs baron before the cocky squads up high could even arrive. A tad embarrassing for them, shall we say?' He rubbed his hands together and gave a wide smile. 'What fun we have together, Shannon. Do let me know when you do your next job and I'll have SOCO standing by.'

'All life is uncertain,' I said philosophically. 'Ask us that after we see how our Friday debrief goes. It's going to be bringing up some awkward issues. Maybe more than awkward, when I think about it. I'd say explosive, but I'm conscious of what happened to Selby. Any progress on that?'

'Not yet, but someone will squeal. Just a matter of time.'

'And the two men under Arthur's van,' I said. 'What joy there?'

'Attempted murder,' Palmer said. 'They're looking at a long stretch. Once they get out of hospital, that is. Right, I'll get out of your hair. I can see you're busy. If you ever need any help . . . don't call me. Best wishes, Cherry. Be lucky.'

He walked from the room and gave a smile. Good for him.

Morag brought us some more coffee.

'This is laborious,' I said to her. 'We need to get a more streamlined way of doing things. We need a system where we can all work simultaneously on one file, access all files easily and get rid of having to email each other with drafts of reports. It's all a bit clanky, if that is a word. Get in touch with Canning, our computer expert at Mid-Anglia Police Force, and ask him what we need. We're level on favours after he helped us on the law job, so we'll pay him a grand. If he won't accept it, tell him we'll make it a donation to the MS Society — his wife is a sufferer.'

Then it was back to the humdrum.

* * *

Anji arrived back at one, which was a good sign, indicating that the biker had made his rounds. She had a triumphant smile on her face.

'It worked!' she shouted. 'The poster trick worked! That cardboard tube stuck out like a sore thumb. You're going to love this. Guess where he went.'

'Do I get three guesses?' I said.

CHAPTER TWENTY

The six of us were sat around the boardroom table set for ten and were all together at one end. The views were amazing, although nobody would have their focus out of the windows. Sir Gerald was at the head of the table with Shapiro to his left. Cherry and I were seated each side and Anji and Valentine one chair away from us, again on each side. There were insulated jugs of coffee and tea on a side table alongside small bottles of still and sparkling water in an ice bucket. I helped myself to coffee, trusting that if it was for the chairman and CEO, it should be better than the weak brew that the masses had to make do with. I carried the coffee back to my seat and let out the breath I was holding.

'There's a phrase in the Bible that we all know,' I said. 'Ecclesiastes 5:10 and 1 Timothy 6:10. "Money is the root of all evil", we think. But that quote is wrong. How it actually reads is "the *love of money*" is the root of all evil. The love of money. Pure greed. That explains egregious actions taken every day around the world. That's what we have to talk about today. The love of money. Let's begin with specifics.

'You called us in because the figures in the Gambling Division made no sense. Now they do. The good news, if we can call it that, is that much of the decrease in profits is down to market conditions — a flagging economy, a decline in discretionary income, all that. When we strip out the extraneous factors, you are performing no worse than your competition.' I took a sip of coffee to moisten my parched mouth. 'Over the course of the last year, you have been milked by a fraud mounted by some of your staff. Would you like to explain, Walker?'

'I'd be delighted, Shannon. It was quite an interesting scam. One of the people who sets the odds in your football department conspired with the watcher to up the odds from that which the computer had calculated. A syndicate, Prometheus, then placed bets on those matches and reaped the rewards when the bet won. It changes the outcomes from being in your favour to being in theirs. Of course, it's a long-term fraud and you need hefty backing at the start and in case of a run of bad luck, but you win in the end. We have calculated the extent of the fraud this year to be in the region of one point two million pounds.'

'My god,' said Campion. 'I think I know what you're going to say next. Our contract with you is for the daily fee and ten per cent of any frauds found.'

'Exactly,' I said. 'One hundred and twenty thousand pounds — here's our final invoice.' I slid the invoice over to Shapiro who read it and showed it to Campion.

'Money well spent, my boy,' Campion said. 'What are the chances of getting any of it back?'

'As I said,' said Walker, 'the syndicate has wealthy backers. I doubt they've spent it all. You could cut a deal. Waive prosecution for getting as much back as you can. It should cover our additional fee several times over.'

'Why should we waive prosecution?' Shapiro asked.

'There's a risk of adverse publicity,' I said, 'and other issues, but we can talk about them later. Let's park that for the moment. You could also check your insurance policy and see if the insurers will cough up.'

I nodded at Walker. 'Carry on.'

'Talking of adverse publicity,' she said, 'there is the more damning consequences of money laundering. Your casinos and betting shops within around an hour or so of London have been taking huge sums of cash and turning that into seemingly clean bank balances. That's why profits are up in London sites and not others — you have punters who haven't cared too much if they lose some money. The launderers will be taking a huge slice of the cash, so some losses hardly matter. My contacts in the Fraud Squad estimate an exchange rate of fifty per cent as standard for the launderers. Every two pounds laundered will become one pound clean for the client. It's a hell of a big business.'

'I don't think there is any chance you can come out of this appearing squeaky clean,' I said. 'That's why on Monday I advised you to start introducing new controls and generating press releases. You might look at capitalising on the successful closing down of a drugs ring. There's a hope in the fact that you acted swiftly and the culprits were apprehended. Worth a shot.'

'And that's where it gets messy,' Walker said. 'We come to the bomb in Selby's car and his resultant death. I think we can safely put that down to the money launderers and the drugs baron — either, or, or both. Our theory is that Selby worked out what was going on, wheedled his way in and took a bribe to turn a blind eye. Then he got greedy and threatened the drugs baron — probably wanted a bigger slice of the pie — "cough up or else I snitch on you." Selby was in deep debt: he needed money desperately or his house of cards would fall down. He became a threat, a loose cannon. He had to be removed.'

Shapiro nodded his head. 'We have everything in hand,' he said. 'We'll work alongside the police and go public when they think it's time. We're in their hands — mustn't do anything that will jeopardize the trial.'

I refilled my coffee. It was better than I had expected, and I needed the caffeine.

'Anji,' I said. 'Time for exhibit A.'

She opened the top of the long cardboard tube she had been carrying, took some Blu-tack from her bag and stuck the poster on the wall. The female tennis player, in all her glory and fame, scratching her naked backside.

'The cardboard tube is important,' I said. Anji waved it in the air for all to see. 'Tell them why, Anji.'

'The only address for the syndicate that we have is a post drop,' she said. 'Picking up the post is the only weak point in the system. The syndicate collects it regularly. When post arrives for them, a motorbike rider picks it up and takes it up the next level in the chain. We can't find the address of where it goes without following the rider. How do we know when the bike is about to make a delivery? Bear in mind, there could be multiple riders or one rider making multiple deliveries. So, here's the clever bit. We send the poster to the mail-drop address. It's too long to be put all the way in the saddle bag, so the tube sticks out. We have our rider. But where does it go? Luckily,' she said with pride, 'I am the only one with a motorbike licence. A car could have been used, but it might have been too obvious or couldn't follow the route of the bike quickly enough. So I took up the chase.'

'Back to the syndicate,' I said. 'It has five members — Fenton and Walters are the inside duo from football, and should be sacked immediately and should be referred to the Fraud Squad, and there are three backers. Valentine, will you do the honours?'

He exited from the room and there were raised voices. Then the door opened and Valentine ushered four women inside — Rose, Violet, Petunia and the Lady Livia herself. Rose in her mutton short skirt, Violet of the startling eyes, Petunia in her carefully chosen safe outfit, and the Lady Livia, in a flowing dress that was more suitable to a ball than a business meeting: the matriarch without whom nothing could be done. *Now is the time to assert yourself, Sir Gerald.*

We had arranged the meeting with the four women on the pretext that Sir Gerald was to make a big announcement.

Which was true in its way, although not the announcement of his retirement that they were hoping for.

Rose immediately saw the poster and her face, even with all the make-up, turned white. The poster was identical to the one the motorbike rider had delivered, and clearly, it was familiar to her. She knew that the game was up, so they say.

'Please be seated, ladies,' I said. 'The fun starts in a moment.'

Campion and Shapiro looked at me in disbelief. What was going on?

'So where did the biker take you, Anji?'

'To the house of one Rose Campion,' she said.

'This is your dilemma, gentlemen. The syndicate has five members, we've heard that already, Felton and Walters, and the three backers, Rose, Violet and Petunia. They stick together like glue. What, sir, do you want to do?'

There was a long pause before anyone said anything.

'Sir Gerald and I need to talk,' said Shapiro. 'Excuse us.'

They left the room, placing us in an awkward position. If there was a prize for the most hated person in the universe, I would have won it hands down.

'I suppose you feel proud of yourselves, you and your cronies,' the Lady Livia said. 'Why must you interfere? Look what trouble you have caused. It could have all been good, all as planned, and then you come along, Shannon. Poking your tedious nose into matters that don't concern you.'

'Fine speech,' I said, 'but you should not be thinking of me. You should be working out what to do to appease Sir Gerald and Shapiro. All three resign for a start, and see how much you can repay. A touch of humility would go down well, too.'

'You're an odious man, Shannon,' Livia said. 'May I never see you again. Now, I think we four need to talk.'

She stood up and, like a mother hen, pecked at the heels of the chicks until they were outside. I hoped she didn't come across Campion.

'Well, that went fine,' I said to the troops.

'Could have been worse,' Walker said.

'In what way?' I said.

'I'm still working on it,' she said.

'Is it always like this?' Valentine asked.

'Goes with the job,' I said. 'Just hope they don't shoot the messenger. No problem with the invoice. They'll get plenty of money back, I think, way enough to cover our fee. There will be a second-hand Porsche to sell, for a start. Tempting, but I think I'll stick with the Beamer.'

'Hard to think that in a moment it will all be over,' Anji said. 'It's been on our minds for two weeks. A daily slog and no room for anything else. It's going to seem very empty.'

'We move on to the next job,' Walker said, 'and the hamster wheel starts turning again. But we've had some fun along the way. Personally, I'd rather do this than anything else.'

'Agreed,' I said.

'Me, too,' said Anji.

Valentine was quiet.

People started to drift back in and return to their seats. Sir Gerald spoke first.

'This is what we offer you. Take it or leave it,' he said. 'Your contracts of employment will be cancelled as from today. Be better if you could be noble and resign, but you will leave this building, never to return. We will not pursue anything with the police.'

Lady Livia nodded her head, seemingly accepting the sackings.

'Furthermore,' Sir Gerald said, 'you will repay what you have stolen. Remortgage your homes, sell your second homes, cash your savings, whatever, but you will repay the lot, every single penny. I will give you a legal document to sign, maybe staged payments, maybe a lump sum: we can sort all that out in due course.'

I interrupted. 'What I would like to know is why? You surely are all well off. I've seen your houses. You must have masses in the bank. Why get involved in this?'

'Am I allowed to say it was fun?' Rose said. 'Bucking the system. Stick it to the man.'

'Who, in this case, is your stepfather. I think you will see a changed man in Sir Gerald from now on. It won't be such an accepting man you'll see.'

Campion nodded his head. Lesson learned.

'I think, Livia,' he said, 'that I would like to talk with you at home. Please take your three daughters from the room.'

They made an undignified exit. Good riddance.

'This has been a fascinating journey to tread,' he said. 'I am eternally grateful. Not just for the money we will get back, but for the diligent way in which you have worked. An example to everyone. David and I have worked out ways to go in the future. We have an offer for you, Nick. We would like you to join the board as a non-executive director — two days a month, one for board meetings and one to read all the papers that precede that. You will be paid handsomely. What do you say?'

'I'd say I am flattered, and I need some time to think. How would it affect our business?'

'Come on, Shannon,' Walker said. 'Accept it. We can cope without you for two days a month — might even be a nice break. Shake the man's hand. You'll love it.'

I stood up and walked to where Campion was sitting. He placed his stockinged feet on the floor and stood up to meet me. We shook hands — double hands. It felt good. 'Welcome,' he said.

'I have to thank you in a personal capacity,' said Shapiro. 'You have transformed Valentine. I've never seen him so full of life. So productive. You have all been mentors to him. Shown him that you can be honourable when conducting business. You give us back a man who is ready for promotion.'

'As this is about me,' Valentine said, 'I reckon I deserve an interruption. Dad, I don't want to come back. If I come back, the charges of nepotism will hang over my head for ever; I will never get respect. And, above all, it's a drag. You should be able to have some fun in your working life. That's what the last two weeks have been.'

'So, what do you want to do?' his father said.

'I want to do what Shannon does. I've never been so happy.'

Shapiro leaned back in the chair and stared at the ceiling. Deep thoughts happening.

'I tell you what we will do,' Shapiro said. 'We will pay your salary for three months, if Shannon takes you on. Maybe after that you can find a comparable job. How does that sound to everybody.'

'If I take Valentine on,' I said, 'it won't be because of the money; I reject that. I will take him on because he is highly intelligent. Because he is a lateral thinker and that is a gift. Because he works hard and is fun to work with. Because he will be an asset.'

I looked at Walker and she nodded.

I looked and Anji and she nodded.

'Welcome to the fold,' I said to Valentine, getting up and shaking his hand to seal the bill.

'You start at the same level as Anji started, with a significant increase after three months if all goes well, and I don't see why that shouldn't be the case. HR — that's Morag — will sort out the details. Over to you, Sir Gerald.'

'I declare this meeting closed,' he said.

And that was how it ended.

CHAPTER TWENTY-ONE

We gathered at Toddy's that evening for a celebratory dinner. Norman, as I have said, always kept a table free until eight o'clock in case we needed it. Which we certainly did that evening.

The restaurant had been closed for four days for a little freshening. The walls were now duck-egg blue with table linen in royal blue — I was glad it wasn't pink like at the Delice. It had a cool feel to it — cool in a sensory way rather than the word Valentine and Anji used. No complaints about that, they kept us up to date with current trends and the possibilities of social media — I don't know my Tik Tok from my WhatsApp. They kept us young. If you can keep someone like Norman young, then that's quite an achievement.

'If we carry on growing like this,' Norman said, 'I'll have to get a bigger table. Maybe even a bigger restaurant. Drinks, everybody. Champagne to start is in order.'

'What news of your van, Arthur?' I said.

'Not worth repairing, but I'll get something as payment from the insurance company. What a palaver that was. Try filling out a claim form for what happened. Drove over two bikers, one with a gun. There wasn't a box to tick for that.'

'Buy a new one and let us know how much,' I said. 'The business will cover it. Keep whatever you get back from the insurers. I don't suppose it will be very much — it was an old van, after all.'

'I loved that van,' he said. 'We'd gone through some great times together. Like losing an old friend, it'll be. Life's not going to be the same.'

The waiter brought three bottles of champagne. Poured one, which didn't go very far among the eight of us. He opened the second bottle, topped up our glasses and put what was left of that bottle and the unopened one in the ice bucket.

'Raise your glasses,' I said. 'A toast to Shannon Investigations.'

We all raised our glasses and took a sip of our champagne.

'And another,' Cherry said. 'A toast to our latest recruit. Valentine.'

Valentine blushed. 'I don't know how to say this . . .'

'Ah, get away with you,' Anji said. 'We all know that. The pleasure is ours. I'll be watching you like a hawk on the next job. Foul up, and I have a punishment in mind for you.'

'I think it's time for us to move on,' I said.

'Not yet,' Cherry said. 'We have a toast still to do. To our new member of the board of Zeus. To our director. Nick.'

It was me blushing this time.

'Morag,' I said. 'May I have the presents, please.'

Morag dipped in her cavernous bag and passed the special contents to me.

'Bonus time,' I said. 'Here's something for each of you. Five grand and we'll pay the tax.'

I passed the cash to each of them. 'For your input in the face of adversity. For you sticking together in times of crisis. To you all. Cheers.'

'What about me?' said Cherry. 'Don't I get anything?'

'Only joking,' I said, passing the last bundle across to her. 'This should keep you in shoes for a while.'

'What is it about shoes that you keep going on about?' Cherry said.

'Shoes,' I said, 'are the mirror of a person's soul. If you see one woman wearing ballet pumps and the other wearing stilettos, you think differently about them, make different judgements. So, to prove I'm not sexist: if you see two men attend a business meeting one in lace-up shoes and the other in flip-flops, you form different views about each of them. Always look at the shoes.'

'Any more advice for everybody?' asked Anji.

'Don't trip over the dead bodies,' I said. 'We seem to have a knack of rustling up a corpse on every job. Words of wisdom over. Let's order. I'm starving.'

Valentine looked puzzled. 'Do you mean I can keep this?' he said, looking at the money.

'Look,' said Norman, 'I'm the one who's usually painted as being stingy — I like to think I'm not stingy, but careful. But that's by the by. We made our usual fee at Zeus, plus a hundred and twenty thousand pounds for the price of uncovering the fraud. What are we supposed to do with it all? Stick it in the bank so we can see it in the accounts and gloat over it like Scrooge? Put it in the safe and count it every morning? You all put yourselves on the line for this job. Any one of you could have jacked it in. Every one of you, I stress. So, every one of you deserves a bonus. Spend it unwisely. End of speech.'

We ordered — I went for a simple green salad with a dill oil dressing for a starter and rack of lamb with vegetables and Toddy' famous triple-fried chips — hence the light starter.

How would I spend my bonus? There was a Cartier Santos watch with gold screws that I had promised myself for a long time. The five-grand bonus would only cover half the price, so the rest needed to come from savings. It would be worth every penny. I wanted something that would remind me of what we had faced in this job and of Cherry's salvation. It would be a watch full of memories.

When the starters had been cleared away, Cherry looked at me. She passed her bonus across to me. 'Get that watch you've always been promising yourself, Shannon. I don't need any new shoes. Hate to know what you would have thought of me whatever I chose.'

God, how lucky I was to have her. And every one of them, too. I was humbled. I added my Cherry's bonus to mine. Pushed it all back over to her.

'What's this?' she said.

'Weddings are expensive nowadays,' I said. 'Here's something to start you off.'

'Does that mean . . . ?' she said.

'Most definitely,' I said. 'Just pick the day. Make me the happiest man in the world.'

Norman leapt to his feet and shouted to the whole restaurant. 'Champagne. Champagne for everybody. On the house. We have a forthcoming wedding to celebrate.'

Waiters scurried around. Buckets filled with ice were laid out by each table and there was an explosion of corks and jollity. We raised our glasses and gave a toast to marriage and then settled back to less exciting things.

'Your father phoned today,' said Morag to Valentine.

'I listened in,' said Beryl. 'No use being a snoop without some snooping.'

'He wanted to send you all good wishes,' Morag said. 'In the couple of hours since he'd last met you, I sensed he wasn't able to vocalize his thinking without getting emotional. He said to tell you he was proud of you.'

'I can't believe it has only been two weeks since we started,' Valentine said, just about managing to keep from welling up. 'I get shivers just thinking about it. Oh, how green I must have seemed.'

'You got that right,' said Norman, 'but from the chrysalis we get the beautiful butterfly.

'Two weeks and my life has changed. My father has never said something like that to me. Encouraging, yes, but never with his heart in it or any thought that I would meet expectations. I can't get over how much my life has changed in those two short weeks. My father's pride touches me. And I've got a bonus to spend.'

'What will you spend it on?' I asked.

'I've seen this cool pair of trainers.'

There was me thinking about a ten grand watch and he had set his heart on a pair of trainers. The age gap widens.

Our mains arrived and there was a lull in conversation as we each savoured our choice.

The rack of lamb was excellent as was everything.

Time to close the door on this adventure.

CHAPTER TWENTY-TWO

It was two weeks later that I got the call. Campion had a box in the Royal Enclosure at Ascot and would like our company. He had a horse running in the third race and it would be a special occasion for him. He'd really love it if we could join him.

I gave Morag the date and time of it, and thought nothing more at that stage. Nothing wrong with a day at the races. Then she dropped the bombshell. There was a dress code — waistcoat and tie, no cravat or bow ties — who the hell wears a cravat nowadays? — black or grey top hat — ditto — and black shoes with socks, which I could cope with. For women, fascinators are not allowed, whereas a hat is. There was a rule about the length of a dress or skirt and other things to wear or not to wear — most of them picky. I asked Morag to send Cherry and me a link.

'I've booked you an appointment with a tailor in Savile Row,' she said. 'A choice of top hats will be there, too, from the company that specializes in them. Basically, I've blocked out the whole day.'

'I forgot to ask you,' I said, 'any acknowledgement of our post-debrief presents?'

'Shapiro loved the framed photo of the selfie of Valentine with Anji in her leathers, and Campion raved about the black leather clogs in the wide size with no back. There is an email about it on the system. Canning took Beryl and I through it and what it does. It will be fantastic when we get past the learning curve.'

I had yet to get acquainted with the new system and asked Morag to keep me two hours in the diary so I could explore it with Beryl sitting by my side for the full induction course.

'Canning wouldn't take the money,' Morag said, 'so I donated it to the MS Society, like you said. I got the receipt sent to him. He said you and him should meet up soon. He owes you a dinner at his house, he said.'

'Can you fix it up with him?' I said. 'Remiss of me.'

A few days later our badges and car park pass came through, and our excitement started to mount. Could be an unforgettable day. May be the only racing day that Campion had left. He was right in saying it would be special.

* * *

Come the day, we were ready to go. Beryl took pictures of us in our finery. I was wearing the obligatory uniform of black frock coat, silver tie and top hat. It suited me, the assembled masses said. Could so many people lie at the same time? My confidence returned to its customary level. I felt like Lord Snooty from the *Beano*, a comic book character from my young days. Cherry had on a long white dress made from silk, cut on the bias, she told me — I don't have a clue either — with dark blue piping around the top and bottom matching her hat. The dress had lace sleeves and it covered her shoulders, thereby meeting the dress code for women. I checked my watch and saw we were running on schedule.

Ascot is in rolling countryside in Berkshire around seventy miles from Docklands. The roads approaching it are prone to traffic jams, so we set out allowing ourselves two hours for the trip. Cherry said she would drive so that I didn't have to worry about holding myself back when drinking with Campion.

The course was laid out as a straight stretch and a triangle, which place to start depending on the length of the race. There are two main areas to view the racing: the Royal Enclosure for the elite and the Grandstand for the not so privileged. The Grandstand had the bookmakers with their screens displaying the odds and the equivalent in percentages. The Royal Enclosure's betting was on a variant of the Tote called Totepool, with kiosks to make your bets. All the money from the bets go into a pool and the winnings are shared out equally depending on the number of winners. With this system, you don't see any odds, but the number of bets on each horse are displayed, so you can get an idea of which horse is the favourite and then down from there.

We parked easily in a specially cordoned-off area and made our way to the gates. We bought race cards — all the runners and riders for each race — and walked to the entrance to the Royal Enclosure. The steward looked at me and patted me down in case I was the world's best-dressed assassin. Satisfied, he mellowed and showed us the way to the boxes, where we would find notices telling us which one was ours.

Our box was high up from the track and had — like the others, I presumed — a commanding view of the action and the finishing post. The box was half full when we arrived and was laid out with lots of ice buckets containing champagne. Waiting staff buzzed around topping up glasses and offering weird and wonderful combinations of canapés. There was no sign of Campion. My heart skipped a beat, hoping that he was well.

We studied our race cards and I saw that Golden Boy was running in the first race — seven furlongs this time, which would be less tiring than the mile he had ridden when we backed him in the betting shop. I couldn't miss having a chance of keeping faith with him. Cherry liked the name of Moonlight Blues: I pointed out to her that you shouldn't choose a horse by its name: you should study the form. She asked me why I was backing Golden Boy. I capitulated.

We set off to the betting kiosks. The odds on both horses had to be worked back from the amount of money staked on each. My guess was that Golden Boy was about 8/1 — eight to one in the old style of expressing odds — and Moonlight Blues a rank outsider, not given much chance at all. We placed fifty pounds each way on each of them. Providing our horses were placed in the top three, we would win money — if either won the race, we would win a hefty sum.

We watched the race through the huge windows from inside Campion's box and, simultaneously on video screens. Golden Boy hung back this time and put on a sprint with two furlongs to go. He lasted well but was overtaken in the run-in. By which horse? Moonlight Blues. Cherry tried to keep an I-told-you-so look from her face and failed miserably.

We had cleared nearly fifteen hundred pounds and decided to leave the buffet that was being laid out for the atmosphere of the Grandstand. Here there were plenty of bookmakers to choose from, as well as the Tote. We chose our horses and went along the line of pitches of the bookies with their odds shown on-screen and sorted out the best odds.

We weren't so lucky this time. At least I wasn't. My horse was placed fourth and Cherry's was second. She should still get a good return for her each way bet, though.

There was a chorus of groans from behind us. An announcement went up from the public address system. The winner had been disqualified for excessive use of the whip.

'What does that mean?' Cherry asked. 'Does my horse win the race now?'

'The best answer I can give is that it depends. It depends what terms and conditions our bookie has. There's no hard and fast rules for what happens after a disqualification. There are a few options. Firstly, the bookmaker makes the bets void and you just get your stake back. Secondly, the bookmaker may have laid down a first-past-the-post rule: even though it was disqualified, the horse *was* the first past the post: the bookie would pay out. Thirdly, another bookie may promote the second-placed horse to be the winner. In which case you will win. We need to find our bookie and see what he does.'

Our bookie operated a first-past-the-post system. Our first piece of bad luck of the day.

The next race was the special one for Campion. I could see him in the ring talking to the trainer and jockey. He was waving his hands around as if giving his instructions. Only serve as confusion, I thought. Leave it all up to the professionals.

The horse was called Lucky Lady and I wondered if there was any significance in the name. Was the horse named after Livia when she had exerted control? Certainly hadn't been lucky lately.

Cherry and I went down to the parade ring, got a bird's-eye view from the rails and examined each horse as it did its circuit. Campion saw us and raised a hand. 'See you later,' he shouted.

The race was over one mile and the form said that Lucky Lady was out of her class, but that wouldn't stop Cherry and I from backing it. We laid our fifty-pound bets at the Totepool, as it had proved lucky in the first race. Lucky Lady was third down in the rankings and I estimated the odds to be around 6/1. We'd each show a profit if the horse was placed and a great return if it won.

The race was a tight one. A lot of horses moving up and down the field as the race progressed. Any one of them could win it. Which we didn't. Lucky Lady came a creditable third. No disgrace in that, considering the opposition.

We collected our money from the kiosk and moved back to the box for some delights from the buffet — some cold roast beef, coronation chicken as we were in the Royal Enclosure, hot onion bhajis and other favourites from around the world. We finished just as Campion came in. He looked, naturally, crestfallen.

'Put up a damn good show,' he said, sitting down next to us. 'She'll be ready for the next race. Tiptop form by then.

Back it. It will win next time, for sure. I'll let you know when and where. What's the time, my boy?'

I checked my watch and told him nearly four o'clock.

'That won't do,' he said.

I checked my watch again. 'Nearly four,' I said again.

'The watch will never do. We can't let you go to your first board meeting with a cheap watch like that. Give it to me.'

I took off the watch and gave it to him. He gave it a passing look. Dropped it on the floor. Stamped on it, the glass shattering and little cogs rolled on the glass. 'Try this one,' he said.

He handed me a package. I was bemused.

'Go on, open it,' he said.

Inside some deep red wrapping paper was a box. Inside the box was a Cartier Santos watch with the gold screws. While I stood there stunned, Campion gave a present to Cherry. Same wrapping paper. Same Cartier Santos watch, but in a smaller women's version.

'I'm touched,' I said. 'I don't know what to say. How did you know what I had promised myself for years?'

'A little bird told me,' he said.

'Does that little bird happen to wear a skater's skirt and black leather biker boots that go over the knee?'

'My lips are sealed,' he said, 'but you forgot the crop top. Now, I hear there's a wedding coming up. See if you can fit me in — I would be humbled.'

'You'll be on the list,' Cherry said. 'No question about it. We can't thank you enough.'

'How's life?' I said.

'Could hardly be finer. Livia and me have an under-standing — I won't boss her around if she won't boss me. She's been a changed woman since the exposure of her three daughters. In shame, I would think. Concerning the three stepdaughters, I haven't seen hide nor hair of any of them, which suits me down to the ground. What a terrible bunch they are. It's like robbing your own family. We've got back half of what is owed with more to come when cars are sold and finances are disentangled.'

'And how's your health? Cherry asked. 'Gout still a problem?'

'It comes and goes, my dear. I'm learning how to manage — bag of frozen peas on the joint seems to do the trick, plus lots of ibuprofens.'

'And you're keeping heathy?' I said 'No other problems?'

'Fit as a fiddle,' he said. 'Zeus has a key staff policy for me. Had the annual medical examination last week. Passed with flying colours.'

His face was open, untroubled: clearly, he wasn't lying to keep up appearances. Cherry and I looked at each other. We were both thinking the same thing.

Crafty old Livia!

THE END

THE JOFFE BOOKS STORY

We began in 2014 when Jasper agreed to publish his mum's much-rejected romance novel and it became a bestseller.

Since then we've grown into the largest independent publisher in the UK. We're extremely proud to publish some of the very best writers in the world, including Joy Ellis, Faith Martin, Caro Ramsay, Helen Forrester, Simon Brett and Robert Goddard. Everyone at Joffe Books loves reading and we never forget that it all begins with the magic of an author telling a story.

We are proud to publish talented first-time authors, as well as established writers whose books we love introducing to a new generation of readers.

We have been shortlisted for Independent Publisher of the Year at the British Book Awards three times, in 2020, 2021 and 2022, and for the Diversity and Inclusivity Award at the Independent Publishing Awards in 2022.

We built this company with your help, and we love to hear from you, so please email us about absolutely anything bookish at: feedback@joffebooks.com

If you want to receive free books every Friday and hear about all our new releases, join our mailing list: www.joffebooks.com/contact

And when you tell your friends about us, just remember: it's pronounced Joffe as in coffee or toffee!

ALSO BY PAUL BENNETT

NICK SHANNON THRILLERS
Book 1: DUE DILIGENCE
Book 2: COLLATERAL DAMAGE
Book 3: FALSE PROFITS
Book 4: THE MONEY RACE
Book 5: BLUE ON BLUE
Book 6: SHANNON'S LAW
Book 7: SHANNON'S GAMBLE

JOHNNY SILVER THRILLERS
Book 1: MERCENARY
Book 2: KILLER IN BLACK
Book 3: ONE BULLET TOO MANY
Book 4: NO EASY WAY OUT

STANDALONE NOVELS
CATALYST